THE ARCHAEOLOGY OF
A DREAM CITY

Balestier Press
Centurion House, London TW18 4AX
www.balestier.com

The Archaeology of a Dream City
Copyright © Monica Raszewski, 2021
Cover image and photographs copyright © Jane E. Brown, 2021

Cover design by Sarah and Schooling

A CIP catalogue record for this book
is available from the British Library.

ISBN 978 1 913891 06 0

This book is a work of fiction. The literary perceptions and
insights are based on experience; all names, characters, places,
and incidents either are products of the author's imagination
or are used fictitiously.

Monica Raszewski

THE ARCHAEOLOGY OF A DREAM CITY

Photographs by Jane E. Brown

Balestier Press
London · Singapore

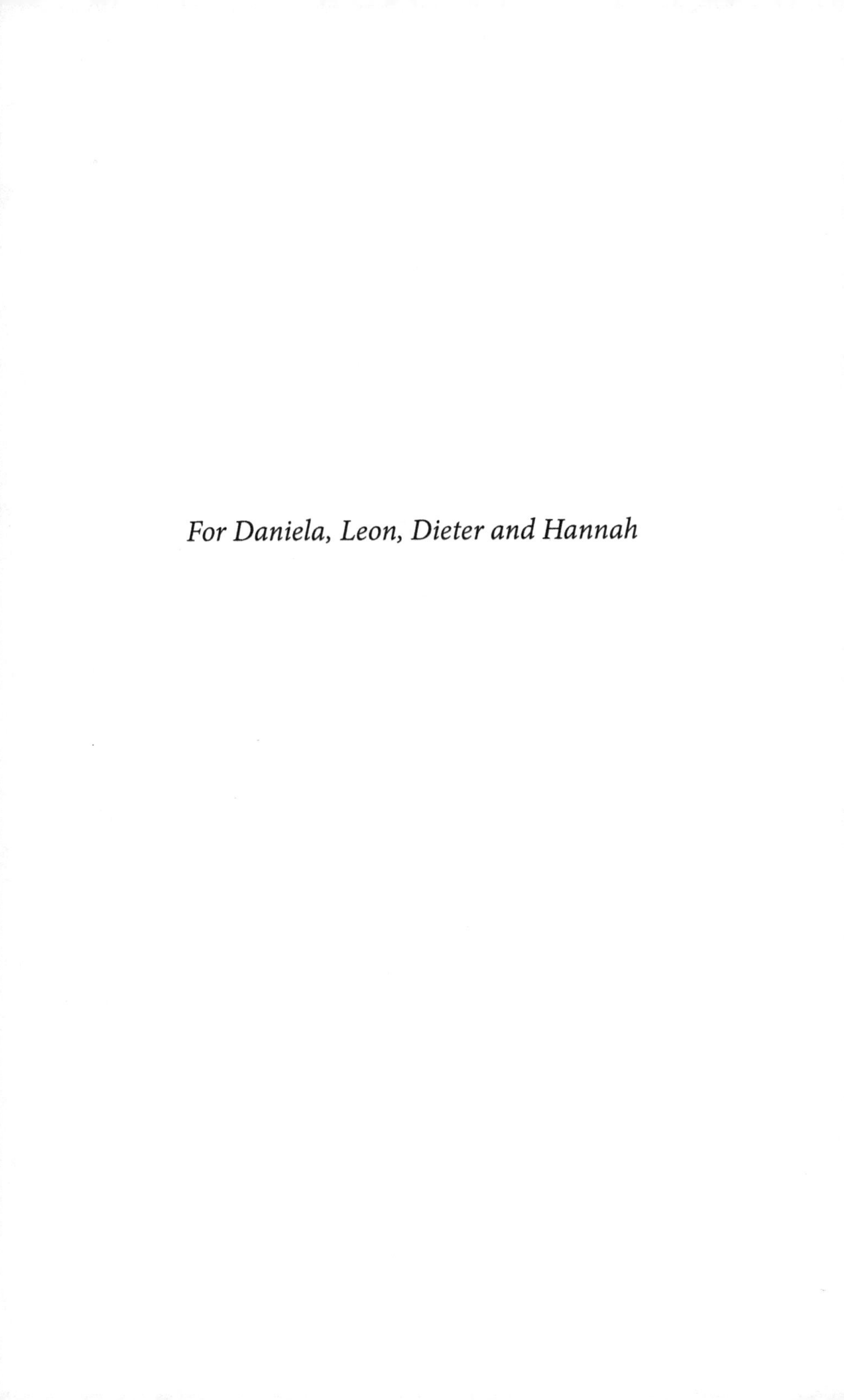

For Daniela, Leon, Dieter and Hannah

Contents

I

En Route

The notes Martha had written about Marion Porter were stacked on the desk in front of her. Marion Porter was a little known but respected Australian photographer active in the 1920s and 30s. Martha had set aside the morning to start writing but hadn't written a word. Instead, she looked out the window at the top of the wooden fence separating her place from next door. The morning light reminded her of summer mornings at her cousin's place on the outskirts of Nadwodom. She used to spend hours lying on the grass in the small back garden with her cousin, Klara, the day stretching before them, discussing what to do; Klara usually suggested, and Martha always agreed.

On the desk beside the pile of notes was a copy of *Marion Porter's Countrysides of Czawa*, a travel narrative with over 500 photographs published in 1937. The book had long been out of print and hard to come by but when Martha finally found a copy, she flicked through it to see if Marion had been to Nadwodom. Martha's father came from that city and her mother had lived there as a very young woman. Most of her relatives on her mother's side still lived there. Marion's trip had lasted three months. Many of the regions she'd visited were now in different countries, and large sections of the population had disappeared, either as a result of Nazi crimes or forcible relocations during or after the Second World War or subsequent migration. Marion Porter visited Nadwodom for only a few days before returning home. She described the city as a modern but rather strange mill town. It was a major textile centre and the busiest industrial centre in Czawa. A third of the population was Jewish, a third was made up of Germans and Russians, and a third were Czawians. She included two photographs of the main market and two photographs of the Jewish market. The Jewish market had narrow alleys lined with closely spaced, covered wooden stalls and was unlike anything seen elsewhere in Czawa. Marion wrote that it reminded her of markets in Damascus. Martha had yet to work out when exactly Marion had been to Damascus, whether it had been on her way to Czawa or whether she had just seen photographs of the market. Marion's book included several photographs of Nadwodom's main market, and she wrote about the huge quantity and variety of foods and merchandise, ranging from boxes of apples and oranges from abroad to live poultry, oil paintings, flowers, scarves, and neckties. The final photograph in this section was of a Jewish stall holder wearing a fez, sitting on a stool beside all kinds of brushes and brooms. He had a beard, wore a long coat and was gazing at the ground a couple of metres in front of him.

In one of the few articles written about Marion Porter, the writer said the photographs Marion had taken in Czawa in the 1930s were full of an uneasy tension that seemed to be a premonition of the coming war. Martha leaned over the desk and opened the window. An ache in her chest grew like a hairline crack, gradually widening and deepening. She had promised Klara that she would return in two years and two years had already passed. The hairline crack grew wider. Martha had wanted to stay in Czawa for a long time. Klara said Martha should stay for at least six months. They talked about a project they could work on together, something that involved taking photographs of the gateways, courtyards and facades of old tenements and abandoned factories, but they never got any further than this.

Martha picked up an article she had printed out and skimmed the first few pages. It discussed the series of photographs Marion had taken of windows and interiors. All the commentary about these photographs mentioned the passage between inside and outside, between the secrets of private existence and the expectations and possibilities of the outside world. No critic ever wrote that the photographs contained a world hidden from view, that they hinted at something beyond what could be seen and that they encouraged dreaming and looking into shadows.

~

For the last seminar in her final year at university, Martha was supposed to present a paper on Baudelaire and translation. Her paper ended up being mainly about a poet from Czawa. When it was time for her presentation, she had stood at the front of the room gripping the typed pages, staring at the words and sentences as if seeing them for the first time. Strings of words bumped into sentences she must have written but could not recognise. The tutor sat on the edge of a table with folded arms, looking down at his shoes. Martha looked over at the grimy window then began to read. Her tongue felt thick, and her mouth swollen. She doubted whether anyone except Tom had ever heard about the poet from Czawa. After stumbling to the end of the first page, she looked up at the floating dust particles that formed a kind of veil across the room. Everyone seemed a long way away. The only person she saw clearly was Tom. He looked at her with large sad eyes, like a saint on a Byzantine icon. He stared and waited. She took a breath and then without pausing or looking up, read to the end. The tutor nodded then pushed himself up into a standing position. He muttered something about turning a crevice inside out then wanted to know where she had found a reference to that image. She leafed through the crumpled and damp pages as if expecting to come across the reference at any moment knowing there was nothing there. The tutor let it go. There were only two other questions and the tutor answered them both. No one asked about the poet from Czawa. Martha retreated to the back of the room, gathered her papers and books and shoved them into her bag.

Tom wished her paper was longer and that she had spoken more clearly. He said that her voice had seemed muffled and that she'd even looked kind of blurry. He thought it might have been all the dust in the place, and that next time she should have water with her. Martha shrugged. In two weeks, she would be on her way to France, and from there, to Czawa. They had sat on a wooden bench outside the library. As they talked, Martha played with a tightly folded piece of paper wedged between the slats. She pulled at the wad of paper and said that what she'd written wasn't properly worked out. The tightly folded paper was still stuck so she tried to push it down through the slats. Tom said he liked the part about silence being like swimming in warm water in the middle of the night. Martha kept fiddling with the wad of paper and said she didn't really know why she wrote what she did. Even though that section didn't fit with the rest of the paper, that was what she saw and felt – a still lake at night with warm water against her skin. She wanted to say that when she was a child and was told to go outside when there were visitors, she would creep back inside and hide behind the couch. Crouched on the floor, she listened to the rhythm of voices, to the sound of the conversations, and when the stories gathered momentum and the voices grew loud, she closed her eyes and let herself be swept up and carried by the rush of sound as if inside a huge wave.

That afternoon Tom had told her about an English translation of new writing from Czawa he'd found in the library. Martha wrote the title and details in her notebook and said she'd try to get a hold of it. She pulled at the wad of paper until it finally gave way then tapped the bench with it as if it was a playing card. She pushed the paper halfway between them. Tom looked at his watch. He had to meet someone about a writing project. They both stood up. Tom quickly picked up the paper and put it in his pocket.

Martha and Tom had become friends after a tutorial in which Martha had not said a word. They had walked out of the building together and spent hours wandering around the city. From then on, they often met up for coffee or lunch. One afternoon, they had walked to Martha's share house. She wanted to cook the orange-ringed mushrooms her parents had given her over the weekend. It must have been a good year for mushrooms because they had picked buckets of them in the pine plantations not far from where they lived. Her housemates had been suspicious when they saw the brightly coloured mushrooms but agreed to try them. Martha took ages to clean and dry the mushrooms while Tom chopped onions and then prepared a rice dish. He was good at cooking and worked fast in the kitchen. Martha sliced the mushrooms then cooked them in butter with onions, sour cream, and lots of pepper and salt. She put a loaf of sliced rye bread on the table and told her housemates that the dish was a delicacy only possible at this time of year. She watched the others as she ate. Only Tom ate more than a couple of mouthfuls. Someone said that the mushrooms were very rich, too rich, and that they preferred the rice dish. Everyone seemed to prefer the rice dish. Even Martha preferred the rice dish.

Tom stayed the night but after he left, they didn't see each other for several days. Over the next few months, they saw each other less often and for shorter periods. When they did get together, Martha spoke fast, as if to fit as much as she could into their conversation. That meant she only heard herself talking though, so she slowed down and left unsaid most of what she wanted to say. At that time, she started working three days a week at Europa, a travel agency with a shop that sold books, magazines, jewelry and gifts from Central and Eastern Europe. Her mother's friend who worked in the travel agency had got her the job. The manager of the gift shop was a fast-moving, squat woman called Elena. When Elena found out that Martha was going to Europe in winter, she warned her about the cold, "When I was fifteen, both my ears nearly fell off because I didn't want to wear a hat with ear flaps." She told Martha she would have to make sure she had the right clothes. The next day Elena brought in a long brown sheepskin coat edged with golden, yellow and red embroidery. She steered Martha to the back of the shop and told her to try it on. Martha put her arms into the thick sleeves then ran her hand over the fur collar. Elena said the coat fitted as if it had been made for her. Martha put out her leg to admire the embroidery and the fur edging. It was the kind of coat a woman seated in the back of a horse-drawn sleigh racing across a frozen lake would wear. Martha paid Elena a hundred dollars and promised to look after the coat.

During her time working at Europa, Martha never knew what she would be asked to do. Sometimes she dusted and rearranged vases or the various carved wooden boxes. Sometimes she ran errands. Sometimes she checked inventories or wrote publicity blurbs. One afternoon, Elena told Martha to stand outside and hand out leaflets advertising a sale of amber jewellery. Martha went into the street and thrust a few leaflets at passersby. After a while there was a lull, so she leaned against a lamp post and gazed down the street. From a distance, she saw a short stocky woman with stiffly coiffed, brass-coloured hair coming up the street. It was an old family friend, Mrs. K, dressed in a light blue knitted skirt and matching jacket. Martha was about to duck into the shop when Mrs. K called out. Martha pressed the leaflets close to her chest. Mrs. K wanted to know what Martha was doing standing out on the street like that. She demanded to see the leaflets. After she read through one, she chuckled and told Martha to buy some amber for herself because it was good for the thyroid and helped with speaking. Then she continued on her way to Myer department store.

Martha went back into the shop and looked at an amber pendant in the display case. She wondered whether it was possible that a lump of amber pressed against her throat could make her speak more clearly. Elena appeared beside her and gave her a cloth. She told her to dust the wooden boxes and then the racks of music CDs. Martha carefully took down all the boxes on the first display shelf and put them on the floor beside her. She wiped down the glass shelf then sat on a stool and picked up a box to dust. A man wearing a brown sheepskin coat and a cap with ear flaps entered the shop. He had come in once before when she was at the counter. That time, he had worn a hat with a red feather in it. He had raised his hat and asked if she had any pictures of the Papa or any saints. Martha didn't know what he was talking about, but Elena rummaged in the cupboard behind the counter and pulled out two icons painted on wood. She held one picture in each hand and rested them on the counter like two shields. The man bent down so that his eyes were level with the pictures. He examined each icon then shook his head.

"The Papa," he said. "You know, the most holy one."

The shop manager got a framed photograph of the Pope, but he shook his head and wagged his finger then he turned to Martha and wagged his finger at her as he left the shop. Martha asked who he was. Elena shrugged.

"Don't know where he's from, something wrong with him, always comes in here when it's cold," she muttered.

This time, the man in the brown sheepskin coat went straight to the step ladder that stood beside the tallest display case. He climbed the ladder and picked up a tall crystal vase. He put the open end to his eye and surveyed the shop like the captain of a sailing ship looking through a telescope. He pivoted around and peered at Martha. She hunched and pushed the cloth into the grooves of an intricately carved box. The man climbed down from the ladder.

"The light, this is the light, you know, the light," he said. Martha looked at him and said she didn't know what he meant. He put the crystal vase to his eye again and said, "The light is the beginning of all things and the light will show the way. It is white light, but you have to know where to look for it, you have to learn how to see it." He held the crystal vase up again and pointed the bottom end at the door. He held it at an angle allowing Martha to look into the open end. There was something about him that reminded her of Tom. She leaned forward and looked through the vase, moving around as he turned it. All of a sudden, a blurry shape moved towards them. While she was trying to focus on the blurry shape, the man whisked the vase away and Martha saw Elena marching towards them. The man put the vase down and rushed out. "He's crazy that one and next time he comes here I'm calling the police."

A month before Martha left for Europe, she moved back into her old bedroom in the family home. The drawers in her desk still contained old high school papers and there were two faded posters on the wall that she had put up when she was seventeen. Everything had been just as she had left it and she took care not to disturb anything, only touching surfaces she could not avoid. She slept in the bed and went in and out as if the room belonged to someone else, some teenager she didn't care about. The teenager that had lived in that bedroom first came across Baudelaire when she studied 'L'Invitation au Voyage' in high school. She sat at her desk and chanted the lines over and over, linking each word to the next so that a never-ending chain of sounds rolled out of her mouth. Then she slumped over the open book, rested her head on her arms with her eyes closed and breathing in the smell of the page, *luxe, calme et volupté*, she walked along a dark, wood-paneled corridor to a room with large windows and a balcony overlooking a river. Velvet couches and mirrors with gilded frames, the luxurious loot of empire, lined the opposite wall. At the end of the room there was a heavy crimson curtain, and behind that curtain, just out of reach, there was an even more magnificent room.

At the back of the wardrobe, Martha discovered her old doll, Lala. The doll had arrived in a parcel from Czawa among books, slippers and packets of dried mushrooms when Martha was seven. The doll had long brown plaits and a folk costume sewn onto her body. Martha tried to get the clothes off, but they were stitched on. The following day she took the doll to school and stood before the class during 'Show and Tell':

- This is my doll, Lala. She came by boat in a brown parcel. Well, her clothes are sewn on, but I can get the top off.

- *Thank you Martha. That's a lovely gypsy costume she's wearing.*

- It's not gypsy.

- It looks just like a gypsy skirt and blouse.

Martha took Lala to school every day.

- This is my doll, Lala. She lives in a tree at the bottom of the garden. She eats soup made from leaves and seeds.

- And what have you got to show us Timothy?

- This is my doll, Lala. The other day she climbed over the fence. She climbed into trees and no one could see her and then she jumped from tree to tree.

- We've heard a lot about your doll, Martha. Maybe you can bring something else to show us tomorrow.

- This is my doll, Lala. Today she had to swim down a big, rocky river. She took off her clothes and left them on a rock.

- Bring something else in next time.

- This is my doll, Lala.

- We know.

- She slept in a tree…

- Not again.

- She gathered acorns and nuts to make soup.

- The gypsy doll again, Martha. I think it is time you had a rest from 'Show and Tell'.

- It took ages for Lala to come. We weren't even sure that she would get here. My grandmother sent her from Czawa. My grandmother is very sick in a hospital.

The children in the class were sick of the doll.

- Thank you, Martha.

Martha took Lala up the street to show Angela. Angela's father was at home with his old friend. Martha could see the long, old-fashioned, white sports car at the top of the driveway jutting out onto the pavement. Angela's mother usually left the house when her husband's old friend arrived. Sometimes the man would call Angela and Martha, then take out his wallet and tell them to go and buy lollies. They knew they were supposed to take their time, so they walked to the milk bar, considering how many lollies could be bought with the money they had and what they would buy. They took a long time choosing the lollies, taking turns, making sure they had a good variety. Then they would saunter back, each holding a brown paper bag pressed to their chests. They usually stopped at the church halfway between the milk bar and Angela's house, sat on the porch step and examined the lollies in their bags. Eventually they picked out a musk stick or fruit jelly and waved it in each other's faces before stuffing it into their mouths.

That afternoon, Martha kept her doll close to her side under her arm. When they finished eating their lollies, they walked back to Angela's place and looked into the white sports car parked at the top of the driveway. The doors were unlocked, so they got in. Angela sat in the driver's seat and Martha sat beside her. Angela pretended to drive, and Martha imagined them rocketing down the driveway, through the garage and out the other side over the hill past the shops. After a while, they got out of the car and sat on the verandah. They could hear horse races being called on the radio and occasional shouts from the men sitting at the table smoking and drinking beer. When they walked in, Angela's father called them over. He seemed happy. He asked to look at Martha's doll. Martha didn't want him to hold Lala too long, but he laughed and threw the doll into the air. He caught her and threw her up again. Martha wanted to catch Lala, but she kept her arms stiffly by her side as she watched the doll fly into the air higher each time until she couldn't stand it, and with her arms still by her side, kicked the coffee table.

Angela's father laughed. He held the doll in both hands as if it was a ball then finally handed her over.

There was a large white vinyl album on the coffee table. Angela opened the album and showed Martha some coins in the clear plastic pockets. She said they were very old, thousands of years old, and that people from the Roman Empire had actually used the coins. She pointed to a large dark brown coin. It was a coin with Nero's head on one side and a chariot horse on the other. She said that he had been the cruellest emperor of all the Roman emperors, that he caused a fire that burnt down the whole city and killed hundreds of people by giving them to lions to eat. Martha peered at Nero's profile on the old, worn coin looking for signs of cruelty. She nodded and squirmed. She wanted to see more of the album and to hear more of the stories, but Angela's father leaned over her and pulled the album towards him. He put his arm around her waist while he turned the page to show her more Nero coins. Martha didn't like the smell of beer or being held so tight. She stood on one leg and with Lala under her arm wriggled out of the man's grasp.

For a long time, Angela did not believe that Czawa existed. When they were younger, they often played with a set of tiny painted wooden dolls at the base of the large overgrown pittosporum at the bottom of Martha's garden. The lower branches of the tree drooped to the ground and formed a kind of cave. Crouched at the base of the tree, low to the ground, they moved the four tiny dolls over protruding roots into and around and over indentations at the base of the trunk. Martha jumped two of the dolls to a cottage in a dense forest not far from an old city with buildings that had balconies and bright orange roofs. The tiny inhabitants of the cottage lived on the mushrooms and berries that grew in the surrounding forest. Angela moved the other two dolls over the exposed roots to a place called Taggerty.

These dolls lived in a farmhouse, where the mother doll had nine children and they ate rabbits for dinner. When Martha heard this for the second time, she grabbed the dolls Angela was playing with and marched them back over the largest protruding root, then through tunnels and caves to Nadwodom. She said, "Everyone is going to Nadwodom." The name rolled out of her mouth as smooth as a pebble. Angela sat up and leaned forward, towering over the dolls. She breathed through her mouth and asked what that word meant. Martha marched the dolls further around the tree trunk and made a little indentation where one of the roots stuck out of the ground. She said that her grandmother and grandfather lived in Nadwodom.

"No such place," Angela said.

Martha piled up dirt and leaves into a mound. Angela leaned over Martha; an intense sweet smell, a mixture of red lollies and mucus, came from her mouth.

"There's no such place," she said again.

Martha said there was, and Angela said there wasn't. They continued like that until Martha pushed Angela aside and ran to the back door. She wanted her mother to come out and stand before them and say that there was a place called Nadwodom and that she would tell them where it was, but no sound came from inside. Martha called again, then stood close to the back door with her ear pressed against the fly wire, as though listening to a voice deep inside the house. She ran back to Angela who stood with her back to the tree and her hands on her hips. She told Angela that her mother said there was a place called Nadwodom in a country called Czawa and it was where her mother grew up and where everyone she knew grew up. Angela shrugged and said she would ask her own mother. Martha shouted in Angela's face in the language that her family spoke to one another. She shouted that Angela didn't know anything, that she was dumb.

Angela pushed Martha back and told her to speak properly. Martha grabbed Angela by the shoulders and they both fell to the ground. Martha kicked hard, so hard that she was nothing but legs kicking. Angela disentangled herself, got away and ran back home crying. Martha sat up and ground her hands into the dirt. Now, her mother stood by the back door waiting. Martha ran back to the tree, pushed through the leaves and squatted close to the tree trunk.

Before she went to kindergarten, Martha and Angela played almost without speaking, since they couldn't understand each other's language. Angela was already in her first year of primary school when Martha went to kindergarten. Mrs. K's husband had given Martha a large old scooter he had picked up from somewhere and fixed up. It was too big for Martha to ride herself, but she and her mother rode it to the kindergarten together. Martha stood in front and reached up to the handlebars while her mother stood behind and steered. Sometimes her younger brother sat on the plank over the back wheel. They sped down the hill until they came to the main road, then they jumped off the scooter, crossed the road, jumped back on and raced down the rest of the hill. The street flattened out and they turned into one street then another until they came to the forest. They went through the forest and emerged into another side street. There was a low red brick fence and then the gates of the kindergarten. Martha had no idea why she had to go nor what she was supposed to do nor what anyone else was doing. She just knew that the other children knew more than she did.

A big old carriage stood in the centre of the play area. One afternoon, Martha found herself outside with a small group and, like a young horse, ran to the carriage behind the leaders. For the first time, she kept running and squeezed through the door of the carriage. She was the second last to make it. Several children remained outside. Some climbed onto the roof and hung down, looking into the window. Inside, there was talk about who would be let in and who would have to get out. Martha sat silent as a stone and kept her spot. When they all clambered out of the carriage, Martha ran beside a girl, and as they ran, they called out to each other. At the end of the day, Martha climbed up onto the low red brick fence. She skipped along the top of the fence and chanted in her mother tongue: I knew what they said – they knew what I said, I knew what they said – they knew what I said.

A few days after Tom mentioned the collection of contemporary poetry from Czawa, Martha borrowed the book from the library. She lay in bed and skimmed through the pages, intending to read an extract here and there before reading the poems properly. She skipped through poems about night and death, lingered over a poem tracing a stone sinking into water, then noticed on the blank last page that someone had written a couple of sentences in pencil. The handwriting was very small: 'Speaking to you is an erotic experience. But who is the you who knows me?' She reread the words and saw that the 'you' in the first sentence could be 'god'. She could not be sure. It made just as much sense if the 'you' was 'god'. 'Speaking to god is an erotic experience. But who is the god who knows me?' Or maybe it was 'Speaking to you is an erotic experience. But who is the you who knows me?' She read these words as if they were a message to be deciphered but couldn't make sense of them. She thought of Tom, and then of the man in the brown sheepskin coat. The person who wrote the sentences in pencil would have written them late at night when the words of a poem or short story set off thoughts that could have branched in any number of directions. She didn't know who wrote on the blank last page or why, but she thought of it as a kind of mysterious omen. Although she was going to meet Angela in Paris, and they had arranged to travel to Nice to do the language course at the University and then planned to travel to Italy and Holland and perhaps England, her real destination was Czawa in the other 'lesser' Europe. She was leaving it for last. It would be like walking along the well-made, well-paved, well-marked roads that led to the rich exciting places everyone knew, then veering aside to a series of small paths or tracks that might peter out or lead to wild forests and bogs, and finally come out who knew where. All she really knew was that she would get there in late spring, that people were waiting for her and that she would stay throughout a long, long summer.

On her last day of work at Europa, Martha came home with the brown embroidered sheepskin coat. Her mother wanted to know how much she had paid, then made a sucking noise. She examined the coat and said it would definitely keep Martha warm and was well made. Martha shoved the coat onto a kitchen chair, then went to the stove, lifted the lid off a large pot and breathed in the smell of cabbage rolls in tomato sauce. Her mother wanted to know what had happened in the shop and who Martha had seen. Martha answered vaguely and said she would help with the rest of the dinner. While she peeled the potatoes, she looked up and caught her mother staring at her, examining her face as if wanting to read her thoughts, see inside her brain, decipher her feelings. Martha put the potatoes into a pot of boiling water then took the plates out of the cupboard and put them on the kitchen bench. Her father came into the kitchen half an hour later and rifled through the cutlery drawer. He asked Martha about her travel plans. She said that Angela had finally heard from the boarding house in Nice and everything was organised.

Her mother frowned. She had never liked Angela's parents, and actually she had never liked Angela either, but she hoped it would go well for them both in France. She drained the potatoes and dished them out. Martha's father set the table then sat down. He had never left Australia since he first arrived in 1959 and had no desire to go anywhere. Whenever his wife suggested a trip, he would shrug, saying he was happy to stay home and would look forward to his wife's stories when she returned.

After dinner, Martha's father peeled an apple and cut it into quarters. He offered a piece to his wife who said that surely by now he knew she didn't like apples. Martha shared the apple with her father while her mother listed the contents of a parcel she had sent to Czawa a few days ago. She hoped the parcel would arrive just as Martha arrived, but even if it didn't, at least Martha wouldn't have to carry presents. She stopped speaking mid-sentence and looked down at the table as if she didn't know what to do next. Martha chewed and swallowed her last bit of apple then asked to see some photographs. Her mother nodded and left the kitchen. As a child, Martha had looked through the photographs in her mother's album dozens of times. She had pored over photographs of a girl with very large brown eyes and dark curls dressed in short frilly dresses and found it hard to think of the girl as her mother or her mother as the girl. The girl in the photo album led, and continued to lead, a separate, independent life. She found it easier to think of her mother when she looked at the pictures of a young woman with short curly hair sunbathing by a river or playing volleyball or sitting with a group of friends, but even then, when the resemblance to her mother was clear, it was like looking at photographs in an old magazine.

Anna, Martha's mother, returned with the photograph album and opened it to the first page. Inside were photographs Martha knew by heart. There was a photograph of her mother as a baby taken a few months before the Second World War began. She lay on a large white cushion and was held semi upright by a young woman with dark hair. The young woman looked down at the baby and the baby stared straight into the camera with strangely large eyes. Then there were the photographs of her mother as a girl, her aunts as girls, her grandparents soon after they married. Martha's father got up and went to the pantry. He came back with a block of chocolate and slid it across the table to Martha. She broke off a piece and peered at a photograph of her mother taken just before she had migrated to Australia. She was on her way to a resort town to meet friends by the river. She sat on her Jawa motorbike and smiled at the camera like a film star from the 1950s. Anna liked to mention that her group of friends included actors and directors from the well-known film school in Nadwodom who later went to America and became famous. Martha broke off a row of chocolate and put another piece into her mouth. Her mother pointed out herself as a girl with skinny legs and said that she was always hungry when she was a child; skinny and hungry during the war and skinny and hungry after the war. During the war when the family living in the house next door was told to leave and new people moved in, Anna knew to keep away. She was not to go near the fence and she was never to speak to them because terrible things could happen. Sometimes Anna watched the two little girls playing in the yard. They had nice clothes and talked loudly in their language. One afternoon, she saw that both girls had a chocolate bar each. Anna watched the girls slowly eating chocolate until she couldn't stand it any longer. She called out to them. She wanted a taste of the chocolate. They stopped eating and stared at her. Then the older girl slowly walked over to the fence and held out her chocolate bar. Just as Anna reached for the chocolate, the girl drew it back, licked it from top to bottom, and then took a bite. Her mouth was covered in chocolate. It was unclear what happened next, because whenever Anna told the story, she swore at the girls in a way she couldn't at the time. Sometimes she said she picked up a fistful of dirt and threw it into the older girl's face, then turned and ran, and at other times her mother ran out, scooped her up and carried her into the house.

Martha carried the sheepskin coat upstairs to her old bedroom and placed it beside the nearly full backpack. She stood at the window and looked down at the garden. Two lime trees grew in place of the big straggly old pittosporum that she used to climb after school. Often, she climbed the tree and balanced on the highest branch she dared stand on, to look beyond the neighbouring gardens and streets at a distant orange tiled roof surrounded by a patch of green. It was the roof of a nineteenth century mansion that belonged to a private girls' school, but when eight-year-old Martha gazed at the bright orange roof and small tower, she saw the top of the oldest palace in Czawa. At that time, she and Angela spent hours sitting in the cave of dark green foliage at the base of the tree talking over their plan to run away. They stored small packets of sultanas and lollies close to the trunk and around the protruding roots in preparation for the night they would meet beneath the tree, climb over the back fence and creep past the neighbours' house into the main road.

Martha turned away from the window and looked at the dusty bookshelves opposite the bed. She searched for a book called *Peoples of the World in Colour*. Her father had given her the book when she was sick with tonsillitis, and she had spent days looking through it. The book had a bright green, glossy cover and illustrations of the Eiffel Tower, a Spanish Flamenco dancer, a man in a gondola and a bagpipe player. Martha turned to the chapter on 'Central and Eastern Europe'. There was an illustration of young women and men dressed in colourful costumes dancing and three musicians playing a cello, a violin and a trumpet. The text described Czawa as a country of hot summers and cold winters. "In the south, it is hilly and wooded, and in the east, there are extensive areas of sparsely populated marshlands and primeval forest. The rest of the country is a vast plain of agricultural and pastureland stretching north to the sea. In the countryside, dotted with villages of painted wooden houses, there is always time for play as well as work. Fairs, market days and religious festivals are fine opportunities for people to wear their colourful traditional costumes, to sing, play all kinds of instruments and dance." On the next page, there was a drawing of a frozen lake with a group of men wearing fur hats and thick jackets holding a fishing net above a hole in the ice. Martha remembered lying in bed with the book beside her, turning her face to the pale blue wall and running her finger along several horizontal cracks just above her head. Her finger glided along the deep and narrow cracks, like an ice skater gliding on ice, an ice skater racing to get home across the blue-white frozen lake while just under the surface the deep cracks, still as fine as hairs, begin to grow wider and wider. The ice skater raced faster as the thick ice behind her began to split open and the gaps grew into black holes.

~

The plane landed at Charles de Gaulle airport at 7 a.m.. Martha pulled the sheepskin coat out of the overhead locker and put it on. She slung her bag over her shoulder and, pressed between bodies, shuffled off the plane. By the time she pulled her backpack off the luggage carousel and heaved it onto her back, she was red in the face, sweating and finding it difficult to breathe. She waddled onto the escalator going down, swayed for a moment, then grabbed the rail. Angela stood below, smiling up at her with bright pink lips. She wore a lightweight jacket and a short skirt. They were new clothes that looked slightly too big. She looked very thin.

Martha stepped off the escalator straight into Angela's arms. They laughed and hugged, then Angela pulled Martha to one side so that she wouldn't block people getting off the escalator. Her hand lingered on the sheepskin coat. "You know it's not cold in Paris. I've been here for ages and I've never been cold." She rubbed lipstick off Martha's cheek then picked up Martha's backpack and carried it to the bus. They sat side by side. Angela described the room she had booked for them in Paris. Martha, still in her coat, said she could hardly believe that the two of them were in Paris together and that in a couple of days, they'd be on their way to Nice. She asked if Angela had heard back from the place they had booked. Angela shook her head and looked out the bus window. She said that she'd decided not to do the language course after all and would stay in Paris. Martha stared at the side of Angela's face. The eye she could see looked at Martha, then Angela turned and spoke as if she was being pelted with questions. She said she had met an Italian man called Sergio a week or so after she had arrived in Paris. Sergio had also recently arrived in Paris and was looking for work. They shared a table in a restaurant and arranged to meet in the same restaurant the following day. They ended up spending most of their time together. Sergio did not have much money and Angela was spending more than she could afford, so they found a room to share. Angela rubbed some more lipstick off Martha's cheek and said she was glad to be spending some time with Martha.

When they got to the hotel room, Martha dropped her backpack in a corner and lay on the bed, flat on her back. Her head was spinning. Angela wanted to go for a walk and a drink, but Martha said she needed to sleep. She lay with her eyes closed until she heard the door close. Then she got up and looked around the room. She opened the wardrobe and saw a small overnight bag. Angela must have left most of her things with Sergio. Martha unzipped the bag and looked inside. She saw a pair of sunglasses, a black lacy bra, black underpants, a silky shirt and a dress. Everything looked new. She zipped up the bag and went back to bed.

When she awoke it was late afternoon and Angela had returned. She had changed into the dress. "Come on. Get up and we'll get something to eat. Don't be so glum. We can still go to Italy like we said. By the way you won't need that coat," she said. They left the hotel and found an inexpensive restaurant. It was crowded but they managed to sit at a table in the far corner. Angela ordered a bottle of wine. Martha looked up from the menu and noticed two young men, one short and plump, the other tall, lanky and wearing glasses, standing in the doorway and looking in their direction. The short, plump man led the way to their table. He asked if he and his friend could join them. Martha nodded and they sat down. The two men lived in London and were in Paris for the weekend. They shared a bottle of wine and then another. Martha ate slowly, like an invalid with no appetite. The shorter man talked and talked. Martha was not sure what he actually did but it seemed he worked with musicians and bands and had an assistant and an office. His friend spoke less, and from time to time turned away from the table as if looking for someone. The short man leaned back in his chair, stretched his arms out and rested them on the back of the chairs on either side of him. He leaned forward and said that Martha reminded him of a singer he knew. Angela's laughter startled the two men. She leaned back in her chair and spoke so quickly that even Martha only caught half of what she'd said, but Martha knew the laugh and understood that Angela wanted to get away from the men. She put her hands on the table and suggested they all go for a walk. Angela glared. They left the restaurant, and the short man walked beside Martha. He said Martha ought to visit London. Martha said she might. She swung her arms as she walked and stared into the lights and into the faces of passersby. She had no idea where she was or where they were going. They eventually arrived at an open space with a fountain in the centre lit by red, green and yellow lights. They sat at a table outside a large café. The short man offered Martha his jacket. She didn't want the jacket, but he insisted so she draped it over her shoulders. The short man ordered drinks. He took a business card from his wallet and wrote his home address on the back. "You can ring me at work during the day. Just leave a message so I know who it is." Martha looked at the handwriting then put the card into her bag. The lights were very bright and the noises around them seemed to be getting louder. She started to feel queasy and a little dizzy. The short man held Martha's hand and said they should meet up the next day. Martha nodded then shook Angela's arm to let her know she wasn't feeling well, that she needed to get back to the hotel. The two of them left the café and walked up a grassy incline. When they got to the top of the embankment, Martha closed her eyes, spread out her arms and fell on the grass. She lay still for a moment, then as if from a great distance, she heard Angela telling her to get up. She opened her eyes. Angela was already halfway down the hill. She scrambled up and followed. Her right foot was hurting from her new shoes. She lagged further behind then stopped and sat on the curb. She took off her right shoe and looked into it. "What are you doing? You can't just sit there. It's too late to just hang around." Angela's voice was high-pitched and sharp. Martha got up and limped back to the hotel.

On their last day together in Paris, Angela insisted on taking

Martha to the Pompidou Centre. She was dressed and ready to go by the time Martha could unzip her backpack. Angela said they would catch up with Sergio at the end of the day. Martha took out her clothes, wondering if the short man would call and thinking that maybe she would go to London after all. She put the card he had given her deep into the side pocket of her bag.

An hour later, they were at the Pompidou Centre standing on the escalators going up. When they reached the top, Martha let Angela go ahead and wandered around on her own in a space that looked like a foyer with video installations and drawings. She scanned the room to get her bearings. A small group of tourists were absorbed in a screen on the opposite side of the room. To her right, a man peered intently at one corner of a huge drawing. He stood so close to the huge, intricate drawing and peered so intently at the spot directly before his eyes, that she would not have been surprised if he stepped into it. He moved to one side to read the display card then moved very close to the wall, detached the card and slipped it under his jumper. He looked up at the drawing for the last time, turned and left. Martha looked around to see if anyone else had seen him. His movements had been so small and quick that she checked to see that the card was gone. She looked at the bit of blank wall and understood the display card contained something of the drawing and something of what the man had seen when he stood before the drawing.

~

The dark green wooden door of the boarding house was locked and there was no one around. Martha knocked, waited, knocked again, then stepped back into the street to see if there was another entrance or a bell she hadn't seen. All the shutters on the lower floors were closed. She banged on the door once again, then took off her backpack and sat on it, holding the sheepskin coat in her arms. So far, she had carried the coat more than she had worn it. She had got stuck in the doorway of the train because of it and had got yelled at by a tiny woman who had somehow walked into it. She had thought of dumping it in some doorway but could not bring herself to do that. She looked down the street wondering if there was somewhere else nearby to stay. After a couple of minutes, she got up, heaved the coat over her shoulder and knocked one more time. Just as she was about to turn away, a thin man in his fifties with a cigarette hanging from the corner of his mouth opened the door. He folded his arms and with the cigarette still in his mouth, asked what she wanted. Martha said she had booked a room from Melbourne, Australia. It was room number three and there were supposed to be two of them but now there was only her. The man shrugged, said he was only the caretaker, squinted, then nodded and beckoned. He went to a cupboard under the stairs and took out a blue-grey blanket and some sheets and then led her up four flights of stairs to the top floor.

The corridor leading to room number three was narrow and dingy, but the room was large, with a window that looked out over a courtyard. The caretaker pointed at the shower recess and drew back the new pink shower curtain. He leaned against the sink, lit a cigarette and said the room had been renovated for tourists. Then he walked over to the bed, patted the mattress and leaned into it. Ash dropped from the tip of the cigarette and floated to the floor. Martha waited while he walked back to the sink, ran his finger along the edge of the stove top and finally walked out. She dropped the sheepskin coat on the end of the bed, shoved the backpack beside the wardrobe then swept up the cigarette ash and opened the shutters. The window opened onto a tiny balcony or ledge just big enough to stand on. Below, in the middle of the paved courtyard, grew two palm trees. One of the palms was small and squat and looked like an open sunshade made of ostrich feathers. The other was almost as tall as the building. Martha leaned to the right. She could just make out the interior of a room on the third floor of the adjacent building. The balcony railing gave way a little. For a moment she imagined falling, arms and legs outstretched, into the furry centre of the squat palm below. She stepped back into the room. The boarding house reminded her of the tenement building she had stayed in when she went to Nadwodom at the age of eleven. She had stood at the large middle window of her aunt's apartment and looked down into the courtyard, at the uneven cobblestones worn down from footsteps made over decades and then at the cracks between the stones, sensing the children that had once crouched over them as they played.

Martha unpacked the cheese and biscuits she had bought in Paris, sat at the table and surveyed the room while she ate. The head of the double bed was pushed against the wall close to the door. Opposite the bed was an old wardrobe with a rectangular mirror set in the door. The only other furniture was the scuffed and rickety table she was sitting at and two chairs. Her mother had once dragged a similar table out of the shed into the backyard of their house. It was the first piece of furniture she had owned in Australia. She rubbed small bits of sandpaper around the edges and blew away the dust. From time to time, she stood back to assess her work and then ran her hand over the smooth wood. She sanded then painted the table over several weeks, stroking it with long, smooth movements as if rubbing down a horse. The table stayed in the shed covered with an old blanket until the day her father pulled it out to use as a sawhorse. The blade cut into the edge of the table once, twice, three times and then the table was never seen again.

Martha licked her finger and pressed it into the last few

crumbs of biscuit scattered on the table. She put her finger to her mouth. Somewhere nearby a woman was singing in Arabic. Martha worked out the sad song was coming from the next room. She got up and stood close to the wall above the sink. She thought her neighbor must be Algerian, maybe living on her own and homesick. All of a sudden, the singing stopped. There was a burst of music then static then some kind of pop song. A high tuneless woman's voice sang along. The pop song cut out, more static, an opera chorus, static. Martha opened the door and looked down the empty corridor. All the doors were shut. She went back to her room and unpacked her clothes then shoved the empty backpack and the brown sheepskin coat into the bottom of the wardrobe.

~

At the University, the teacher for phonetique stretched her lips back and showed a row of white teeth then opened her mouth to form a perfect O. She told the students to open their mouths wide and let the words roll out from inside their throats instead of squeezing them through their front teeth. Martha imitated the teacher and repeated the vowels, imagining a perfectly round hole drilled into a block of wood. When classes finished, she caught the bus back and got off a stop early. She skirted the railway station and walked past cobbled alleys and dingy, dilapidated buildings then walked up the narrow street to the boarding house. She put the key in the lock of the heavy green door, but it wouldn't budge. She took the key out and tried again. After several attempts, she took a deep breath, turned the key and rammed her shoulder against the door. She lurched across the threshold and nearly collided with a pale young woman with very short blonde hair. The woman jumped back and flattened herself against the inside wall. Martha stepped aside and the woman darted out the door muttering *excusez-moi*. Martha noticed that she had bare feet and wore a light cotton dress. The door slammed shut behind her. The caretaker stood on the landing, swinging a bucket. He tapped his forehead with his index finger then shook his head.

The only person Martha had spoken to in the boarding house, apart from the caretaker, was a young man in his twenties called Frank. He lived in a room at the end of the corridor two doors down. They occasionally met on the stairs and spoke a mixture of French and English. Frank boasted that he had taught himself English from books and films and insisted on speaking to her in English. Martha said she needed to practice French so Frank invited her to meet his friends. She walked into his room one evening and saw the pale, blonde woman sitting on a wooden chair balanced on its two back legs. Her toes just touched the ground. Her feet were very white, with a little grime lacing the edges. Frank introduced Odile and said she lived in the room between them. Frank's room was almost half the size of Martha's room but somehow a couch had been squeezed in. Another young man was half-sat, half-sprawled on the couch. He had a narrow, pointed face and small, pointed teeth that reminded Martha of a fox. There was nowhere else to sit so Martha sat beside him. Frank passed around a joint. Martha hesitated, took a puff then passed it on. Odile sat forward and the front legs of the chair banged on the floorboards. She reached down and took a green apple and a small knife out of her bag. She peeled the apple, carefully holding up the long green curl before letting it drop to the floor. She cut the apple into quarters and gave everyone one a piece. Martha noticed a large brown spot in the middle of her piece of apple. She bit all around the brown spot then sat holding it, hiding it in her palm. She asked the young man sitting beside her if he also lived in the boarding house. He grinned and looked at the others as if he didn't understand.

Eventually, Martha learned that he lived on the second floor with his mother and younger brother and he was never going back to the small village in the mountains where he came from.

While the others kept smoking, Martha went to the window, leaned out and without looking down, dropped the bit of apple. It was twilight and the electric blue sky seemed unusually close. It seemed so close that if she leaned a little further out and reached up, she would be able to sink her fingers into it. She turned back to the room and said that the sky here was different; it was a deeper colour and somehow brighter than it was in Melbourne. She tried to describe how she saw the sky, but Frank shrugged and said it was probably the lights from the town. Odile leaned towards Frank so that their heads almost touched, and their lips brushed each other's ears. They whispered and murmured. Martha turned back to the window. If Tom were in Nice, they would have seen the same sky and there would be no need for any description. They would have looked down into the dark courtyards and seen shadows and strange shapes that neither would have had to describe.

That night, Martha lay in the middle of the bed with her arms over the blanket staring at the ceiling. The room was hot and stuffy. She had dozed a little and could still feel the end of a dream where she had tried to pull herself out of a pool of water. No matter how hard she tried to climb out of the water she kept falling back, her body too heavy to emerge onto land. Martha turned onto her side and kicked off the blanket. A scraping noise came from the other side of the room. She stared into the darkness and listened. Slowly, she crept to the sink. The scraping and digging was coming from the other side of the wall. It sounded as if someone was trying to tunnel into her room using a spoon. She crept back to bed and listened until the scraping stopped.

At dawn, a shadow hurtled down as if to smother her. She sat up and waited for a moment, breathing in the thick, heavy, stale air clogged with the germs and smells of each person sleeping in the boarding house. Then holding her breath, she got out of bed and opened the balcony door. She leaned against the rickety little railing and took a deep breath. A light shone from a room on the fourth floor and another from a room on the third floor in the adjacent building. She could just make out the ostrich feather palm below, surrounded by paving that looked like an arrangement of broken eggshells. She went back inside and put her ear to the wall just above the sink. She heard nothing. She filled the kettle, letting the water gush from the tap before realizing the scraping had started again. Now, she was certain it was Odile working at the plaster wall with a fork or metal spoon. Martha tapped on the wall and the scraping stopped. She waited, ready for it to begin again, but everything was quiet. She banged the kettle onto the stove, flung open the wardrobe and got dressed.

Instead of catching the second bus that would take her right to the University, Martha walked up the hill. Halfway up, she turned and looked down at the blue-grey sea, heaving slowly and rhythmically like a blanket covering a sleeping body. On this side of town, there was the sea and there was affluence. She continued walking up the hill, turning every now and again to gaze at the water, murmuring to herself in French, trying out the rhythm of the Niçoise in a kind of sing-song. By the time she got to the classroom, the class had already started. She sidled in and sat beside the least proficient French speaker in the class, who also spoke more than anyone else. Halfway through the lesson, the student nudged Martha and asked what her place was like because she needed a place to stay. Martha answered vaguely and left the University early.

The front door of the boarding house was open, but the building seemed deserted. She met no one on the stairs and heard no sounds. She loitered outside her room and fumbled with the key, no one passed. She looked down the staircase, no one in sight. She went into her room, sat at the table and took out her notebook.

From Frank:

Cinglé – crazy

Foutre le camp – to piss off

J'en ai plein le cul – pissed off

She thought of knocking on Frank's door to see if he was in but knew she would probably end up standing outside his door then returning to her room. She read over her notes from the previous day then skimmed over the list of new words the class had been given. Finally, she lay her head on the notebook and breathed in the smell of the paper. Someone drove a motorbike into the courtyard. Martha lifted her head as the sound got louder and looked out the balcony window. The young man she had seen in Frank's room rode his motorbike around the central palm tree. He circled the tree slowly then picked up speed, getting closer to the tree as he circled it, as if lassoing it with a rope. Then he revved the motorbike, broke away from the tree and sped out of the courtyard.

One morning, while she splashed cold water over her face, Martha heard bare feet running on wooden floorboards. She turned off the tap and put her ear to the wall. Odile was either running on the spot or running up and down the length of her room, muttering and swearing as she ran. A man mumbled and groaned as if he was trying to sleep. Odile shouted, "*Merde, merde, merde!*" The man told Odile to be quiet and Martha recognized the voice of the caretaker. Odile shouted at him to get out of the bed and to get out of her room. The caretaker told Odile to calm down. Odile yelled at him to get out. There was a quiet moment during which the caretaker must have climbed out of bed and got dressed. Then he walked across the room and slammed the door behind him.

Martha went out to the bakery. It had been raining and the pavement was wet and grimy, and every now and then a murky puddle appeared. She kept her eyes down and stepped over dog turd just before she entered the bakery. She bought a loaf of bread and two escargots then returned to the boarding house. The air in her room was warm and stale, as if she had stepped into a big ear. She opened the window and made a cup of tea. She imagined what it would be like to walk barefoot along the cold, wet and gritty pavement. After a while, a thin layer of grime would cover the soles of her feet like a second layer of skin. She put down her cup and put her ear to the wall above the sink. There was a slight movement on the other side and a sigh. Martha held her breath. There was no other sound. She waited for some kind of noise but there was nothing. She picked up the two round pastries she had left on the table and went to Odile's room. After she knocked several times, the door opened a fraction and Martha looked through the crack. The door opened a little wider. Martha could see light shining in through the slats of the shutters and could just make out the shape of a bed piled high with blankets and clothes. She held up the two escargots. Odile stood to one side and opened the door wide. Above the wash basin, in the place where a mirror might have hung, there was a hole in the plaster. A dusty radio jutted from the basin as though someone had tried to ram it down the plughole. Odile managed to fill the kettle without getting the radio wet and turned on the little gas stove beside the basin. She waved at the hole in the plaster and said the landlord often worked on the plumbing but had never seemed to fix it. Martha put the escargots on the bench Odile used as a table and looked around for somewhere to sit. She sat on the edge of Odile's bed. On the floor beside her, there was a small sculpture or model made of cardboard and paper. The sculpture was about half a metre long and reached halfway up Martha's shin. It was a model of a long building, with no roof, divided into several rooms. Each room had a doorway into at least one other room. Tiny red, green, yellow and pink figures stood in doorways, looked through windows or were grouped together as if talking. One of the figures, a woman with a red cap on her head, seemed to have had her head glued to a wall. Odile explained that she had made the sculpture from bits of rubbish and was still working on it. The figures reminded Martha of the small wooden dolls that had arrived in a parcel from Czawa when she was about eight. She crossed her legs, and while swinging one leg over the other, knocked the cardboard building with her foot. All the figures toppled over except for the woman with her head glued to the wall. Odile pounced on the sculpture as if rescuing a child. Martha apologised and tried to set the figures straight. Odile scooped up the cardboard building and pushed it into the corner.

While Odile rummaged in the sink looking for cups, Martha asked if she had always lived in Nice. Odile said she'd been living in Nice for about three years. She had left Paris to go on a holiday that was only supposed to last two weeks but never went back. Her family knew she was living somewhere in Nice but that was all. Odile handed Martha a cup of hot water with a teabag in it and an escargot, then sat on the floor. Martha slowly slid off the end of the bed and also sat on the floor. She noticed that just beneath the ceiling on the wall behind Odile, several black cockroaches were crawling in a line. They had probably made their way down the corridor from the toilet or through people's rooms, most likely heading to their nests in the piles of clothes and rubbish in Odile's room. Odile leaned back on her hands and stretched out her legs. She said that lately she could not bring herself to eat the food she bought from the market because she knew it was contaminated with sprays. She pointed at some red spots on her chin and on her left cheek.

Martha put aside her half-eaten escargot and nodded at some photographs pinned on a board standing in the corner. Odile looked over her shoulder. Martha pointed at a photograph of a girl in a tutu which seemed too tight. The photograph was taken when Odile had wanted to be a ballet dancer, but just as she had begun to make real progress, her mother became worried that Odile would damage her feet. She told Odile that if she practiced too hard, she would break her toes and would not even notice until she took off her ballet shoes and saw her feet covered in blood. Odile got up and took down the black and white photographs pinned to the board. They were taken at the Roman ruins just outside Nice. There was a photograph of the walls and edges of an aqueduct that once ran through bath houses, and another of overgrown stones that used to be part of the amphitheatre. Martha peered at a photograph of Odile and a tall man with long hair. Odile and her boyfriend stood in an open field. The wind blew her boyfriend's hair across his face. He had his hands in his coat pockets and was beaming at the camera. Odile also smiled, and her windblown hair looked like blades of grass. Odile explained that underneath the ruins, the earth was riddled with a system of underground tunnels. The two of them had gone past the no access signs and crept into a tunnel. They followed it into a type of underground cave. Odile left her boyfriend and continued down another tunnel. She said it was like going to the centre of the earth but in order to get out she had to go deeper and deeper. Her boyfriend panicked and called after her. He insisted she turn back but she kept going until there was no sound or light.

The sky was grey and heavy throughout that day. When Martha left Odile, she went downstairs and out the building. She walked fast in the direction of the bus stop. Just in front, a short elderly woman shuffled along with her head down, careful not to trip or lose her balance. As she passed the woman, Martha brushed against her. She felt the slight pressure of the woman's shoulder, then stopped and looked back, worried that she might have knocked her over. The old woman also stopped and looked up. Martha opened her mouth but couldn't think of what to say. She mumbled, *Excusez-moi, excusez-moi, je suis desolée, j'espère que vous êtes…* The old woman muttered under her breath, walked around Martha and entered the bakery. Martha continued to the bus stop. She remembered staying with her grandparents in a town near Nadwodom when she was eleven. One morning, her grandmother handed her a string bag and said they would go to the market together. They went down the stairs and out the front entrance of the block of flats to the bus stop. Martha wore the new boots her mother had bought her for the trip. Her grandfather called and waved from the balcony. Martha waved back while her grandmother ignored him. The bus looked full, but they made their way to the back. Martha sat a few seats away from her grandmother. Two stops later, an elderly man and woman got on at the back door opposite where Martha sat. Martha continued to gaze out the bus door. Then she realised that the elderly couple was staring at her. For a moment, Martha didn't know why they were staring. She blushed and looked behind. Her grandmother glared and motioned at her to stand up. Martha stood, but her thin, too long body and her awkward movements made it seem as if she didn't want to get up. She shuffled towards her grandmother and stood looking down at the tips of her boots, at the floor, at other people's shoes. Her grandmother tugged at her sleeve to let her know they would get off at the next stop. Martha turned in the aisle just as her grandmother stood up. The bus stopped suddenly. Martha lurched forward, her left leg jerked up behind her and she kicked her grandmother in the shin. Her grandmother winced and limped off the bus. They stood on the street and Martha watched the blood seep through her grandmother's stocking.

Martha got off the bus at the Old Marketplace in Vieux Nice hoping to bump into one of the other students. At the far end of the square, a small audience gathered around a high wooden stage that looked like a giant four-poster bed. Reams of light pink gauze were draped over four poles to make a canopy. The gauze was so fine that the edges dissolved against the sky. An actor wearing a black mask and a crimson, gold and green jester's costume clung to the top of a pole at one corner of the stage. Three actors, made up like dolls, climbed the scaffolding beside the stage. The audience pressed close to watch the show and to keep warm. The jester spoke to the audience then twisted around the pole and called out to one of the actors. Martha, unsure if the jester was speaking Italian or some kind of old French, strained to understand what he said. The jester winked, smirked and spun around on the pole. The large mistress of the house flirted with a young visitor. A pale young woman with a rose bud mouth watched her mistress seduce the young man. She crept to the front of the stage, leaned forward and whispered to the audience. Two short plaits stood out on either side of her face and bobbed as she moved her head. She stepped back into the middle of the stage, clasped her hands to her breast and looked from side to side. She stretched out her arms to the audience seeking their sympathy then she jumped and dashed from one side of the stage to the other, running back and forth in what

Martha saw as a make-believe version of a room in a boarding house.

~

After four weeks, Martha stopped going to the University. On the morning she decided she would no longer go to classes, she lay in bed with her arms behind her head and stared at the thin, steel blue blanket covering the sheet. When she first went to Czawa at the age of eleven, she packed the rose-pink dressing gown that always lay on top of her bedclothes deep into her mother's suitcase. For as long as Martha could remember, she had slept with the dressing gown that had once belonged to her mother spread over her doona. She called it Shava and never thought of it as an actual dressing gown. It had a sweet musty smell and was made of a silky-smooth padded nylon. The stitching that held the padding in place had come undone in several places and the padding had either disappeared or become lumpish and able to move around. Martha liked those sections best. She liked to rub the two sides of the outer casing between her fingers. On most mornings throughout her childhood, she touched the cold material when she opened her eyes. Then, with her head still on the pillow, she observed the undulating landscape the rose-pink dressing gown formed on her bed. The bits of Shava she liked least were the sleeves. They reminded her that Shava had once been a dressing gown. The sleeves hung out the side in an ungainly way and were the best preserved. When the rest of Shava transformed into the topography of a country, into valleys and ridges and hills, the sleeves had to be ignored.

Once they arrived in Czawa, Martha kept Shava hidden. Whenever they travelled to different parts of the country, she left Shava behind, hidden at the bottom of her mother's suitcase.

The only time she didn't check the suitcase was when her mother packed their things to return home. There were so many things to take back: embroidered slippers, carved boxes, books, beaded necklaces. Her aunts and her grandparents were all preoccupied with packing the suitcase and another new suitcase. It was only when they arrived in Melbourne that Martha found out that Shava had been left behind and that her grandmother had thought Martha ought to be ashamed of dragging around such an old rag.

Odile knocked on her door and came in. She had a bag of food that she had bought at the market. Martha jumped out of bed and threw on a jumper and trousers. Odile emptied the bag onto the small table. Martha glanced at Odile's black, pointed and well-worn boots. They looked in need of repair. She remembered her father saying that in hard times, a person's most valuable possession was a pair of good, strong boots.

They cut up the tomatoes, cheese and bread and opened the jars of pickled artichokes and olives. They prepared the food and ate in silence. Odile picked up the jar of olives, held the jar close to her chest and put an olive into her mouth. She smiled at Martha as she ate another olive then another. Martha smiled and reached for the jar. Odile moved away. Martha looked at the fat, round olive between Odile's thumb and forefinger as her hand emerged from the jar. Odile held up the olive and slowly turned her hand. Martha made as if to lunge forward and Odile put the olive into Martha's mouth. Martha moved the olive around in her mouth with her tongue. Odile laughed and wriggled her fingers in the air as if daring Martha to bite them. Martha would have liked to bite them hard. Instead, she sat back in her chair and looked away. She stretched out her legs and rested her hands on her stomach. Odile moved her chair closer and also stretched out her legs. They sat side by side facing the window.

To fill her days while she considered what to do next, Martha often went to the old market square and strolled among the stalls selling leather goods and clothes, jewellery and souvenirs. She went from stall to stall, never buying anything until the day she saw her old classmate in the distance. It was the student who had asked about moving into the boarding house. She watched her pick up something, look at it intently then put it back. When the student moved away, Martha approached the stall which sold *commedia dell'arte* masks and other leather goods. Martha picked up a maroon coloured mask with a nose as sharp and pointed as a beak. The cheeks were high and also sharp and on either side of the almond shaped eyeholes there were fine sculpted ripples that looked like plumage. Martha stroked the leather plumage then asked the price. She bargained the way her mother would have done and bought the mask. She put it deep into her bag and decided to catch a bus to the Roman ruins at Cimiez.

The ruins were almost deserted, and it was easy for Martha to avoid the few other tourists. She wandered among the many shallow ditches looking out for tunnels, but there were none that she could see. Alternate stone and brick courses ran in straight lines like miniature roadways with built up sides. They led to a dry and dusty central pool. She zipped up her jacket to keep out the wind and put her hands in her pockets. When she was certain that all the other tourists were in the Matisse museum, she stepped into what was once a pool and lay on her back. The stone edges protected her from the wind. She closed her eyes and turned her face so that her right cheek pressed into the earth. If the ground gave way she would sink deep into the earth, into a dark blue hollow where Odile had stood barefoot in her dirty light cotton dress, her skin so transparent that the blue veins showed through.

Martha knocked on Odile's door with the bird mask behind her back. Odile opened the door and stepped aside. She indicated Martha should sit on the bed. Martha sat on the edge of the bed and placed the mask on her lap. Odile ran her finger along the smooth, hard leather cheeks then picked up the mask and held it in both hands to have a closer look. Martha said she could have it. Odile turned to Martha and peered at her face. She moved so close that Martha could feel her breath. Odile said she could see something moving inside Martha's eyes, a shadow passing behind a glass pane. Martha asked for a cup of tea or coffee or something to drink. Odile put the mask on the bed behind her and said she would make hot chocolate. She put the kettle on the stove, placed two cups on the table and spooned in dark powdered chocolate. Then she dropped a white pellet into each cup. Once the kettle boiled, she poured in the water and added milk. She took a spoon out of the sink and stirred the chocolate. She handed Martha a blue cup with a chip just above the handle. Martha sipped the brown liquid. It had a bitter chemical taste that stayed in her mouth. She took another mouthful and swirled the liquid over her tongue before forcing it down. Odile picked up a magazine from the floor and flicked through it as if searching for something. Martha looked into the blue chipped cup and took another sip. This time she wanted to spit out the liquid. The room was so dirty and cluttered anything could have got into the chocolate or the milk or even the water. Martha said she had to go back to her room because she had left the door open. She took the cup with her and tipped the rest of the liquid into the sink. She rinsed the cup and stood there for a while. She decided to go back and return the cup. Odile was still sitting on the floor with an open magazine on her lap.

She looked up and smiled. She suggested they go to a nightclub. Martha hesitated, but Odile insisted it was just down the street. She went to the wardrobe and took out a green dress with lace sleeves and a white lace dress with a skirt that billowed out in the style of the 1950s. The green dress was for Martha. It smelt of stale sweat and dust. Odile insisted she try it on. While Martha held the dress against her body, Odile changed into the white dress.

"Hurry up, let's go," she said. Martha changed into the green dress and they rushed out of the building. Odile walked down the street fast, pushing past anyone in her way, letting one hand trail behind her. Martha tried to reach the hand but never quite grasped it. As soon as they reached the nightclub, they found themselves in the middle of a crowd. A man and a woman got between them and Martha lost sight of Odile. She pushed through the crowd and stood in a corner looking out for Odile, turning left, right, left, right, like a lighthouse beacon. Occasionally, a white shirt or skirt caught her eye but there was no sign of Odile. The music thumped through her body and she began to find it difficult to breathe. She made her way to the bar and at last spotted Odile talking to a man. Martha waved and Odile beckoned. The man handed Martha a glass of wine. She drank and tried to listen to their conversation. Odile and the man stood very close together. Martha had no idea what they were saying. She drank more wine and her stomach churned. She began to feel hot and dizzy. There was nowhere to sit. She mimed that she had to go outside then pushed through the crowd and ran out onto the street. She waited for Odile and, concentrating hard, tried to quell the nausea. It seemed to her that she had stood there for a very long time before deciding to walk back to the boarding house.

When Martha stood before the green front door, she realised

she had left her keys in the pocket of her jeans. She banged on the door with the flat of her hand then pounded it with her fist. As a last resort, she picked up a handful of gravel and threw the little stones at a window on the first floor. The stones reached halfway then showered down onto the pavement. The nausea and stomach cramps became more intense. Doubled over and holding her stomach, she walked to the other end of the building. For the first time, she ventured down the lane between the boarding house and the next building. An opening off the lane led into the courtyard. Her stomach churned. She leaned against a wall and peered into the dark. Two people sat on the back doorstep smoking. She recognised Frank. He spoke quietly, murmuring something about having to take his friend's motorbike. Martha held her hand over her mouth and lurched towards them. Frank jumped up. When he realised it was Martha, he held the door open and helped her up the step. Then he flicked the butt of his cigarette into the courtyard and sat down on the doorstep again.

The door to Odile's room was unlocked. The stomach cramps were getting worse and Martha just managed to scoop up her clothes, find her keys and rush into her room. She went straight to the sink and vomited. Then she pulled off Odile's dress, threw it on the floor and got into bed. Her head ached and soon, the nausea and stomach cramps returned. She groaned and turned from side to side, then got up, gripped the side of the sink and vomited again. She lowered her head to the edge of the sink. The metal felt like a cool hand pressing against her forehead. The voice belonging to the hand told her to drink lots of water to flush out the poison. She pulled herself up and drank from the tap. A different hand gripped her insides. It let go for a moment then squeezed harder. Martha got back into bed but couldn't lie still. She tossed from side to side, burrowing into the sagging mattress. A door somewhere nearby opened and closed. She began to worry that she might end up sick for days and no one would know. She called out, "*Je suis malade, je suis malade,*" then half-crawled to the sink and banged on the wall.

A doctor came that night. Martha was not sure whether she had been dozing or awake. She lay in the dark, flat on her back. She couldn't see properly but it seemed to her that the doctor wore a mask that covered the top part of his face and a dark cloak so that no one would recognise him. The doctor peered into her face. He gave her an injection then some sweet raspberry gel in a little spoon. She felt nauseous again and half-sat up, but the doctor told her to lie still and wait for the medicine to work. He turned to someone in the room and said that it would just take time. He disappeared. Frank and Odile were somewhere in the room, somewhere in the shadows, she was sure of that. There was movement in the far corner near the wardrobe. She peered into the darkness and saw a pair of glinting eyes. The eyes had a red tinge and were down low, as if the person or creature was crouching. She waited for the creature to come forward. The eyes shone like jewels, like precious stones in the eye sockets of ancient statues. She stared and waited. The eyes stared back. She lowered herself down onto the bed still watching and then the eyes disappeared, leaving the darkness complete.

Sometime during the next day, Martha awoke and knew that the poison had dissipated. She lay on her back feeling light, floating above the bed, wanting to stay like that. There was a knock and the door opened slightly. Frank looked in and held out a bowl of soup. He asked Martha if she was feeling better. Martha sat up and nodded. She pulled the musty bedclothes over her chest and sniffed. She could smell her stale sweat and unwashed hair. She took the bowl of soup and let Frank sit on the edge of the bed. She breathed in the smell of the soup then ate a spoonful. It tasted good. She put spoonful after spoonful into her mouth. There was a knock and the door opened a crack. Frank's friend peered into the room. The caretaker stood behind him then pushed forward. He looked around, sniffed the air and grimaced. Frank asked if she wanted more soup. Martha shook her head then lay back on the pillow and stared at the reflection in the mirror on the wardrobe door. They were all still standing in the doorway, and now Odile was also there, peering in. Her eyes were big and round. Martha turned to look at her. In a loud high-pitched voice, Odile asked Martha if she wanted a cup of mint tea. Martha shook her head, closed her eyes and turned away. Odile said mint tea was good for the digestion. The others told Odile to be quiet and pushed her back into the corridor. Martha could hear her saying that she had done nothing, that she had not given Martha anything bad. She must have worked her way back into the room because Martha heard her declare close to her ear that she would make Martha a cup of mint tea. The door closed and Martha opened her eyes. They had all left. She remembered that sometime in the night Odile had appeared in her room and put a spoonful of sweet raspberry gel into her mouth. The raspberry gel slid down Martha's throat, spreading into the crevices of her stomach, cooling and calming her insides.

The room needed fresh air. Martha got up and opened the window. She took a deep breath. The bright blue sky pressed down on the palm trees and the neighbouring buildings. The courtyard seemed tighter and narrower, and the smaller palm was almost miniature. She decided to leave in the next few days, to book a train ticket to Paris as soon as she could and from there fly to Czawa. It would be the beginning of spring and she would spend several weeks exploring the cities with her aunts and cousins. Once summer began, her aunt would find a place to stay in the country, and Martha, together with her cousins, would spend several weeks living in a wooden farmhouse with a thatched roof and carved lintels at the door and windows. From her upstairs window Martha would have a view of the surrounding rye fields and the clear stream that ran beyond the fields on the edge of a cool, dark green forest.

Two days before she left the boarding house, Martha went to the wardrobe and pulled out the brown sheepskin coat. She went to Odile's room and knocked on the door. She stood in the doorway and held out the coat. Odile stroked the fur edged cuff and said, yes, she would wear it.

~

On the train to Paris, Martha overheard a man reading something from the newspaper to his companion. A conversation started up about an explosion or a fire, some kind of conflagration burning out of control. She couldn't follow everything that was being said but understood that a serious accident had happened, that there was an uncontrolled fire, that somehow all of Europe was in danger.

As soon as she got off the train in Paris, she bought a newspaper and read that two days earlier there had been an explosion in the reactor block of a nuclear power plant to the east of Czawa. She moved away from the kiosk and tried to read the article on the front page. It continued on page six and there were more articles about the disaster throughout the newspaper. She couldn't make sense of it all. She went back to the hotel she had stayed in when she first arrived in Paris. When she got to her room, she locked the door and opened the newspaper. There was a large heading and a brief article on the front page, '*L'accident de la central nucleaire a fait plusieurs victimes.*' Martha read through the article but there was no specific information about who the victims were, or how many, or what had happened to them. She read that the nuclear power plant was one hundred and thirty kilometres north of the capital city and that it was still unknown whether the accident had been catastrophic or not. It seemed obvious to Martha that it was catastrophic. She turned to a map of Europe on page eight. Five black arrows beginning at a black spot representing the nuclear power plant extended over Northern Europe and a thin arrow swept over Czawa. A few weeks later she learned that seventy-five percent of the radioactive fallout drifted north-west over villages and countryside. The radiation was invisible, floating in clouds spreading, unchanged in strength, across the continent of Europe and thousands of kilometres beyond.

That evening Martha phoned her parents. Her mother answered so quickly she must have been sitting by the telephone. She wanted Martha to come home as soon as possible because no one could know how long the fire would burn or what it would mean and her father was very worried, everyone was worried. She really had to come back. Martha's mother said it would be impossible for Martha to go to Czawa and be a burden on the family. It was hard enough for them to live and now it would be even harder to get food; they would be taking food out of their own mouths to give to her. Martha said nothing. To end the conversation, she said she would wait, she would wait and see, but she already knew she would not get to Czawa.

Every morning Martha bought a newspaper, returned to her room and read whatever was written about the nuclear accident. She wondered how quickly radioactivity spread. She wondered how the invisible cloud travelled. She wondered where it went, how far it spread, how high it rose and whether radioactivity would be in the rain. The only thing she knew for certain was that the graphite fire inside the reactor was extremely hard to put out and that it would burn for days, perhaps weeks. Whenever she went out, she looked for Angela but never saw her. Once she saw a woman walking on the other side of the road wearing oversized sunglasses and she had been certain it was Angela, but before she could get to her, the woman disappeared. She kept hoping she would run into someone she knew. At night she lay in the dark thinking how little seemed to be known about the radioactivity around them, how people didn't know what might happen. She thought of an invisible dust seeping into the atmosphere, contaminating everything, entering bodies without anyone knowing. In the morning, she reminded herself not to eat spinach or lettuce. Later, she learned that the glowing core had to be smothered with concrete, sand and lead, that the workers who did this work got sick and died horrible deaths. She learned that the nearby town was evacuated, supposedly temporarily, but that this later became permanent, and that a few days later the evacuation area or exclusion zone was expanded to thirty kilometres around the power plant.

By the fifth night that Martha had spent in Paris, the incongruity between the bright sunny days, where everything seemed to go on as normal, and the dread of the night, when she saw herself standing alone on the street unable to move, became unbearable. The following day she booked her flight to Melbourne, then went to a cafe and sat at an outdoor table. She had spent nearly all her money but ordered a big meal. When the green salad arrived, she piled it onto her plate and ate until it was all gone. Then she sat back in her chair and looked up at the blue cloudless sky.

10
379
HOLEŠOVICE - BUBNY
PRAHA 7

FOTOKO

HISTORISCHE & PROFESSIONELLE
KAMERAS, OBJEKTIVE, ZUBEHÖR

VSTUP
ZAKÁZÁN !

3,1
m
6
MHD
V OBOU
SMĚRECH

II

MOVING IN

On the page in front of her, Martha had written: *Porter's early photographs of windows and interiors capture the uneasy tension, the passage between inside and outside, between the secrets of private existence and the expectations and possibilities of the outside world.* She looked up and out at the top of the wooden fence. If she had been born in Nadwodom and not in Melbourne, then she and Klara would have known each other all their lives. If she had been born in Nadwodom, if she had grown up in Nadwodom, she would have been completely different. If she had been born and grown up in Nadwodom, she would have been more certain, she would have been like Klara; one the shadow of the other. The ache in her chest deepened. Surely a feeling this physical would lead somewhere. The ache travelled up to her throat. She reached over the desk to open the window and stayed a moment, hovering over her papers. Beyond the top of the wooden fence and dark green bushes, beyond the roof of the neighbour's house, was a thin strip of pale blue sky. She wanted to draw herself up, to stretch into the pale blue, as though this would alleviate her sense of constriction. She slumped back into the chair. If she had been born and lived in Nadwodom, she would have lived inside the buildings she had only seen from the outside, she would have known the people that lived there, she would have spent her days writing and reading, she would have had many lovers, she would be assured. The ache moved to her stomach. Like the dragon in the children's book her grandmother had sent her, she could eat the entire city. She was the child that took sacks of rocks to the dragon's cave to trick it into eating them and she was the dragon that gorged itself.

At 9pm on a Monday night three years after Martha returned from France, the telephone rang for a few seconds, stopped, then rang again thirty seconds later. The same thing used to happen whenever Mrs. K rang her mother. Martha pounced on the phone. The voice on the other end sounded like gravel falling on concrete.

"Your mother wants to know how you are," she said.

"I'm fine."

"You haven't seen her for a long time. She's worried you're not well."

"I've been busy."

"Are you looking after yourself?"

"Yes."

"Are you happy where you are?"

"Yes."

"I'll tell her you're busy."

"And how are you Mrs. K?"

Mrs. K was not so well but didn't expect much at her age. She was going to Czawa for four months and wanted to know if Martha would look after her house while she was away. Martha said she would and arranged to visit Mrs. K on the weekend.

On most weekends throughout her childhood, Martha's father drove the family across town to visit either his sisters or Mrs. K. Even though Martha had not visited Mrs. K for over two years she could get to Mrs. K's house without thinking. She drove into the narrow dead-end street then did a U turn just as her father used to do. She got out of the car and looked at the kitchen window. One of the slats of the venetian blinds was being held down by a finger and two large brown eyes stared at the car. Martha waved. The slats flicked back into place. By the time Martha reached the porch, Mrs. K stood by the front door holding the fly wire door open. As Martha approached, Mrs. K held up her hand and said no kisses, she did not want to pass on germs. Martha nodded and said she didn't want to pass on any germs either. Martha carried her bags into the hallway and Mrs. K locked the door. A huge green suitcase lay open in the middle of the living room. Martha walked around it and put her bags in a corner by the couch.

Mrs. K asked Martha to help weigh her suitcase. She closed the lid and pushed down on it while Martha pulled the zip around. Martha noticed her stiff fingers and oversized knuckles; Mrs. K's arthritis must have got worse. Martha heaved the suitcase onto the bathroom scale and saw it was five kilograms overweight. Mrs. K sat on the arm of the couch and nodded, satisfied, then pushed herself up off the armrest and went to the kitchen to make tea. Martha followed her into the kitchen, sat at the table and looked down at the linoleum. The pattern made her think of vegetable salad. She lifted her feet slightly and let them hover over the expanse of green peas, finely diced carrots, potatoes, egg, apple and pickled cucumber speckled with black pepper. Throughout her childhood, vegetable salad had been her favourite dish. She remembered sitting before two large, glass bowls of vegetable salad on Mrs. K's name day and waiting. Her father leaned over a pot of clear red beetroot soup like an alchemist, dipping a spoon into the pot, sipping, inhaling the aroma then shaking his head. Mrs. K passed him the sugar bowl, the vinegar, and half a lemon. She was no good at cooking; she'd never had the time to learn. When Martha's aunt arrived with a tray of ear shaped pastries, Martha carried the bowls of vegetable salad into the lounge room and put one on each of the two card tables covered with linen tablecloths. As soon as she could, Martha scooped vegetable salad onto her plate, flattening the pile so that it looked like a raised plateau rather than a mountain. Then she sat on a stool in the corner and put spoonful after spoonful into her mouth. She concentrated on the crunch of dill cucumbers and apple, then savoured the soft yet still firm potatoes, carrots and peas as they dissolved in her mouth. She let the taste of mustard sauce linger on her tongue then she tried to taste everything at once. She chewed and swirled the food around her mouth, but the harder she tried to grasp the whole, the more the taste eluded her. She shoved spoonful after spoonful of vegetable salad into her mouth until she could eat no more.

From the other side of the room her cousin, Nadia, beckoned and Martha, together with her brother, went outside. Nadia was six years older than Martha. She was three when her family left Nadwodom and she hadn't wanted to leave. On the day they left their apartment, she watched the adults carry suitcases and boxes from the hallway into a black car. She refused to move but she was small for her age and could easily be picked up. She was placed on her mother's knees. Her two older sisters sat on either side of her. She stared straight ahead during the car trip to the railway station and later during most of the train journey to Genoa. From time to time, she gazed out the window but did not speak. An uncle was waiting for them at the train station. He stood with his hands in his pockets and rocked backwards and forwards on his heels. When he saw the black car, he sauntered towards it and helped unload the suitcases and bags. When all the baggage stood neatly stacked on the pavement, Nadia demanded that he put all the bags and suitcases back in the car. On the ship from Genoa to Melbourne, Nadia slept much more than usual. Even when she was awake she seemed half-asleep. One evening, her parents left their children in the cabin and went to the dining room to watch a film. When they returned, Nadia was not in her bunk. They ran down the corridor in opposite directions. Her mother ran up to the deck and saw Nadia standing near the rail at the prow of the ship, wearing boots and her coat buttoned up to her chin. She called out. Nadia turned but did not see her mother. Her gaze was fixed on something just in front of her. Her mother rushed to her daughter and held her tight. Nadia began to cry and to shout. She shouted words her mother did not understand and struggled to get out of her mother's arms. Later, when she was older, she was able to say that her grandfather had appeared. From then on, he appeared at night when she lay in bed. She closed her eyes and saw her grandfather who had died before she was born, walking along a railway line. He was in the distance and walking away but he would stop and look back as if waiting for her to join him.

Martha, her brother and cousin sat on the low brick fence outside Mrs. K's house and faced the factory opposite. Nadia with her long golden hair was the Queen of the Sea. She picked up a long stick and held it as if it were a fishing rod. She let the fishing rod nod a few times, pulled it up, then let it down again until they caught a golden fish. They agreed to let the golden fish back in the water and it granted them three wishes. Nadia was the interpreter. Only she could talk to the golden fish and only she could tell the fish what the wishes were. Martha wanted to speak to the golden fish herself, she wanted to whisper to it so no one else would hear. Nadia shook her head and insisted that Martha tell her the wish. Martha squirmed and looked down, her lips pressed shut. Nadia gave her the fishing rod and said she had to say her wish out loud. Martha couldn't say the words. The wishes were too secret, too childish. She wanted to live in a house on top of a green hill, on the edge of a forest on the other side of a stream where she could look out the window and draw trees and the rooftops of the nearby town. From the top of the hill, she would fly over the nearby town and see everything all at once, then linger over each street and see inside each building and house. Martha sat on the low brick fence with her lips pressed shut. Nadia and Martha's brother turned away then slid off the fence and went back inside Mrs. K's house. Martha walked across the road and dragged the fishing rod up and down the corrugated iron fence. She looked over her shoulder then let the stick drop and dragged it behind her as she went around the corner. It was a hot day and the door to the factory was open. Martha peered inside as she passed. There were two rows of sewing machines and behind each whirring sewing machine sat a woman with her head down, twisting and pulling material through the machine at lightning speed. One of the women had her hair tied up in a red scarf. The woman looked up at her for a split second. Martha hunched her shoulders and skulked away.

The factory building was still there but it was no longer a factory. Martha wanted to ask what the building was being used for, but Mrs. K had her head in the pantry. She took out packets of biscuits, tea, coffee, and breakfast cereals and piled them on the kitchen table. "You don't need to worry about buying anything for a while."

They went around the kitchen and she opened each cupboard and drawer so that Martha would know what was inside. The fridge was packed with food. There were bottles of soft drink, juice, milk, cream, sour cream, yoghurt, vegetables, jars of pickles and several small parcels wrapped in butchers' paper. Mrs. K took out a couple of parcels, opened them, sniffed and showed them to Martha. Then she put them back into the fridge, shut the fridge door and said they would go to Pizza Hut for dinner.

Martha helped Mrs. K into the car then got into the driver's seat and clicked Mrs. K's seatbelt into place. From the corner of her eye, she saw Mrs. K make a quick sign of the cross with her right thumb. When they entered the Pizza Hut, they made their way to a corner table by the window. Mrs. K looked smaller than she did in her house. She gazed at the other tables and her eyes became bigger, softer and a deeper brown. She handed Martha a menu and told her to ask for the pizza with the most ham and cheese and vegetables on top and the thickest base. She said if they ordered a bowl of salad, they could go to the salad bar and fill it up as often as they liked. Martha ordered a special deep-fried pizza, two glasses of Coca-Cola and a bowl of salad. She put down the menu and looked at Mrs. K's hands. The fingers were broad, swollen and stiff. The knuckles were large, a little disfigured and the joint of the thumb stuck out, rock solid and immovable. Mrs. K had worked in a hosiery factory for over twenty-five years and Martha had some notion that she kept her fingers, or maybe even her hands, wet all the time she worked. She pictured Mrs. K seated behind a type of sewing machine, dipping her fingers into a finger bowl as she spun silken thread. Her mother used to say that Mrs. K always wore the best quality lingerie: silk underpants, camisoles, lace trimmed bras. On one of the rare occasions she was not wearing her best quality lingerie, she had been involved in a car accident. That day she was wearing old baggy cotton underpants with holes in them, a torn singlet and a frayed yellow-grey bra. That had been her husband's fault. Instead of helping her paint the kitchen, he offered to take her to the drive-in. She wanted to take a shower and change her clothes but he insisted there was no point because it was already getting dark. She got into the car and just as they turned the corner, another car ran into them. Mr. K's white station wagon skidded across the road and rolled over. Mrs. K hung upside down trapped by the seat belt. There was smashed glass all over the road. Mr. K wriggled out of the car with cuts on his face and leg. The ambulance arrived. Mrs. K was freed and taken to hospital. There, in the hospital, the nurses and the doctor all saw her frayed, yellowed bra, torn singlet and baggy cotton pants with holes in them.

Shortly after the car accident, Martha and her mother went to see Mrs. K. She had two broken ribs and a badly bruised arm. She sat in bed propped up by a large white feather pillow. Her slinky, dark green and black dressing gown was open at the neck and showed the edge of a satin pink nightgown. Martha's mother placed a tray in front of Mrs. K then brought in a bowl of chicken broth. She sat on the edge of the bed. Martha sat on a stool by the dressing table behind her mother. The gold ring, with the dark purple stone that Mrs. K usually wore on the middle finger of her right hand, lay on the dressing table. It was the only thing Mrs. K had from her old life in Czawa. Martha slid her index finger along the top of the dressing table and touched the ring. She pushed the ring a little way, then hooked her finger into the gold band and drew it towards her until the ring plunged off the edge of the table and dangled stone side down. She held the ring between two fingers then brought it up to eye level. She tried to look at Mrs. K through the semi-transparent stone. The ring fell out of her hands, bounced on the carpet and rolled under the bed. Martha's mother glared at her as she picked up the ring.

She reached across, put the ring in the top drawer of the dressing table and slammed it shut.

While they ate pizza, Mrs. K told Martha she would spend most of her time on her brother's farm near a village in Western Czawa. She showed Martha a small photograph of a house with a high-pitched roof and three people standing in the yard. The people were Mrs. K's brother, her nephew and his wife. It must have been a grey, overcast day and the yard looked muddy. Before the war, Mrs. K's family held large tracts of land in Eastern Czawa. When the borders changed, those members of the family who had survived and remained were forced to move across the country and resettle in the newly acquired western border area. The farmhouse Mrs. K's brother and his wife took over had belonged to a German family who in turn had to move further west. More than thirty years later, Mrs. K's nephew began to build a new house on the farm. The house would have a room for Mrs. K with a bathroom next to it. The foundations had been poured and the cellar dug but it would take many more years to finish. Mrs. K packed the photograph back in her bag and said that the house would be built bit by bit, and she would continue to send money so they could buy the building materials they needed when they could get hold of them. Once the house was finished, Mrs. K would sell her house in Melbourne and move to Czawa. Martha could imagine Mrs. K living on some kind of country estate but not on a small isolated muddy farm.

"Really? Wouldn't you find it too cold?" she asked.

Mrs. K pointed at the empty salad bowl and told Martha to go and fill it up. She looked down at her hand with the finger still pointing and said she would spend several weeks in a sanatorium renowned for its healing mineral springs. Martha went to the salad bar, leaving Mrs. K to sit and observe everyone who entered and left the restaurant. She returned with a full bowl of salad and set it down on the table. Mrs. K nodded. She put a few lettuce leaves on her plate and insisted that Martha eat the rest. She took out her house key, slid it across the table and said she was relying on Martha to keep an eye on things, including Hela, a boarder who lived in the back section of the house. Martha helped Mrs. K put on her coat and tried to pay the bill even though she knew Mrs. K wouldn't allow it. They linked arms and went to the car park. Mrs. K made another furtive sign of the cross just before she got into the car and Martha sat behind the wheel as if about to take off in a spacecraft.

When they returned to the house, Mrs. K turned on all the lights and said they needed some good strong black tea to wash down all the muck they'd eaten. Then she showed Martha the bedroom. A single bed piled high with feather bedding stood in the centre of the room. Along the length of one wall was a huge built-in wardrobe and on the opposite wall was a long dressing table. Martha had forgotten that the bedroom was so small. They sidestepped along the narrow aisle between the bed and the wardrobe. Mrs. K opened the sliding doors and they looked inside. The wardrobe was packed tight with clothes, boxes and shoes. Mrs. K tried to squash some of the clothes together then shook her head. She thought Martha might be able to squeeze one or two things in if she could find a spare clothes hanger. They sidled around to the other side of the bed. Mrs. K opened the two top drawers of the dressing table and beamed. She stepped back to show that they were completely empty and ready to hold Martha's belongings.

That night Martha slept on the couch in the living room. The couch was too short to lie flat on, so she drew up her legs and lay on her side with her face close to the back of the couch. She ran her fingers along the grain of the fabric. It had a ribbed texture, grooves then furry raised bits. At first, she tried not to breathe in the slightly musty smell but after a while she got used to it. She closed her eyes and thought of the couch crowded with people, surrounded by people pressed together, sitting on the armrests, on armchairs, on kitchen stools. If someone wanted to get in or out of the room, everyone had to move. They talked loudly, sometimes one after the other, sometimes all at once, sometimes over the top of each other. Aunt Luisa was always in the centre, the funniest, the quickest. Her husband, Uncle Daniel, was often absent from these gatherings. He was either seeing patients in his surgery at home or studying or visiting his sister's family and friends.

When Martha was ten, her mother found a hard lump about the size of a ten-cent piece in the middle of Martha's chest. She didn't know if it was an extra bone or some kind of growth so they went to see Uncle Daniel. Aunt Luisa opened the front door, but instead of putting her finger to her lips and nodding at the surgery door, she opened it for them. Martha and her mother went straight into the surgery. Martha sat on the edge of the high examination table on a starched white sheet and stared at the bone coloured, plastic hand lying palm down on Uncle Daniel's desk. Nadia had once taken Martha into the surgery and allowed her to take off the first layer of plastic to reveal red muscle and veins. Then she took this layer off to reveal fine delicate bones barely touching each other at the joints. While Martha stared at the hand, her mother rolled up Martha's top to reveal the lump. Uncle Daniel peered at the slight protrusion in the middle of Martha's chest then glided the tips of his fingers over it. His fingers were neither cold nor warm, they moved so delicately that Martha could hardly feel them on her skin. He looked into her face, smiled and said that some people just had bones like that. Martha smiled back at him, pulled down her top and jumped off the examination table. Her mother took a deep breath and murmured thanks to God but then asked if the bone could grow. Daniel said there was a possibility, but didn't think so. Martha's mother wanted to know what would happen if the bone did grow. What should they do? How big could it grow? Could it grow to the size of an apple and sit there like a third breast?

Martha did not yet have any breasts and didn't want any. She edged over to the glass fronted cabinet opposite her uncle's desk and looked at a plastic model of a heart. It looked like a lopsided mango and stood on a rod. Red and blue pipes stuck out the top. She placed her fingertips on the glass panel of the cabinet as gently as her uncle had placed his fingers on her chest and slid the glass door across. She touched the pink, grooved surface of the mango-heart. She could see that the top section of the heart could be removed and that there might be several sections inside, but she also knew not to reach for the heart there and then. Before she could make out exactly how the top layer could be prised off, her mother put her hand on her shoulder. They left the surgery and went to the dining room. A large plum cake sat on a cut crystal dish in the centre of the table. There were many glass teacups and a small plate of sliced lemon. Martha's unmarried aunt, Mary, sat at the end of the oval table with the window behind her. She had her elbows on the table with her hands clasped together. Her eyes reflected the cut crystal dish and the crystal bowls on the sideboard. She leaned forward and told a story about a foolish husband and wife that went back to Czawa with the money they had saved in Australia. The man was a fine jeweller but when he arrived in Melbourne, he found work in a carpet factory, and the woman, who was a fine singer, washed dishes and worked as a cleaner. They bought land on the outskirts of Nadwodom and planned to build a villa. Martha's aunt lowered her clasped hands, rested them on the table and took a deep breath. Firstly, the building materials had taken months to arrive, bricks came in dribs and drabs and when the other materials arrived, they had come at the wrong time. Then nearly everything on the building site was stolen. She shook her head. The husband and wife lost nearly everything they had. They returned to Australia a year later, the villa was never built and they had to work harder than before.

When Uncle Daniel finished with his last patient, he entered the room and sat at the other end of the table. He said he learned more from his patients than they learned from him.

"I asked him, where do you prefer, Australia or Czawa? Where was your life better? Here or back there?"

"Ah, doctor, he said, neither here nor there."

"But where did you feel best?"

"You know where I felt best? I felt best on the ship, on the way from there to here."

Uncle Daniel died three years later. His wife and sister-in-law were visiting Mrs. K. They returned that evening and found him lying face down across his desk, one arm stretched out towards the window as if reaching for something.

~

After she had dropped Mrs. K off at the airport, Martha drove back to the house and sat in the car for a moment. The house seemed even lower and smaller than it had the day before. The knee-high gate in the low brick fence looked too narrow for an adult to pass through and even the paving stones leading to the porch seemed too small for an adult sized foot. Martha leaned back in the car seat. She had taken the day off work. She had nowhere to drive to, no reason to move. Ahead of her, a man wearing a tall conical hat edged with fur crossed the road. He strode purposefully, as if on his way to a meeting. Martha watched him until he disappeared behind a building. She felt as if she had arrived in a far-flung part of Czawa, a tiny fragment of Czawa that had split off and drifted away. Mrs. K's ex-husband had lived in the adjoining suburb, and Martha's aunts still lived just a few streets away. The last time Martha visited her Aunt Mary and Aunt Luisa, she'd also had the impression that their house had shrunk. She sat in the tiny kitchen and looked out the window at Aunt Mary's bungalow. After Uncle Daniel died and all the children moved out, Aunt Mary moved out of the bungalow into the room that had been Daniel's surgery. The bungalow behind the lemon tree became a miniature warehouse, packed with piles of newspapers and magazines, boxes, books, neatly folded stacks and rolls of material that could only be glimpsed through the bungalow windows. When the last box and crate were squeezed in, the door was shut and not opened again until Aunt Mary died. The bungalow contained all the things she had put aside for later as well as things she had saved from being thrown out. She had stored all of Daniel's old medical books from Czawa, piles of clothes collected over many years that she planned to pack and send to Czawa or to mend and give to the local Opportunity shop. She had stacks of magazines, newspapers and books put aside for when she'd have time to read. On the day Martha visited, Aunt Mary had sat at the table and declared, as she had many times before, that she simply had no time. Aunt Luisa, who had been standing at the stove frying meat, threw her arms into the air, looked up to the heavens and asked how it was possible that her sister was born with no time.

Martha had only been inside the bungalow twice. When she was about ten, Aunt Mary beckoned and said she had something for her. Martha followed her out the back door and stood on the step below while her aunt unlocked the door of the bungalow. Martha stood just inside. Her aunt edged around a tall wardrobe and disappeared. She rummaged in a box or drawer and then a moment later, came out from behind the wardrobe holding a small doll dressed in a folk costume. The doll was made from some stiff padded material that had faded. The arms were curved and moved up and down at the shoulder. Two long slightly fuzzy brown plaits lay over a white lace collar. The dress had multi-coloured stripes and was covered with a gold apron trimmed with lace the colour of dark chocolate. The feet were in black boots and were nailed into a round wooden base. The nails had loosened over time, so the doll swayed backwards and forwards. Martha put her hand underneath the doll's skirt and petticoat, held her by the legs and tilted her forward. It seemed to her that the doll was not a plaything and she promised to look after it. When they returned to the kitchen, Aunt Luisa gave her a big block of dark chocolate. Martha held the doll in one hand and with her other hand broke off pieces of chocolate then put them into her mouth until she had eaten the entire block. From the moment she left her aunts' house, whenever she looked at the chocolate coloured lace around the apron, she felt nauseous.

Martha got out of the car and stepped over the fence into Mrs. K's garden. Three steps later and she was standing on the porch. She fumbled with the key, pushed open the heavy door and stepped inside. It was cold. She turned on the heater then took her bags to Mrs. K's bedroom. She sat on the edge of the bed and pulled off her boots. Soon after they separated, Mr. K had a minor stroke that left him with a stiff right leg. Mrs. K took him back and they lived together for another two years. He still went away on fishing trips and hunting trips, returning home late at night, filthy, too big for the house, and so exhausted he pissed in the hand basin instead of the toilet. From time to time, he took Martha's family camping. They drove to a large river near the mountains. Once, it began raining the day after they set up a campsite. It rained steadily for days. On the third day of rain, Martha lay on her camp bed and ran her fingers down the tent wall. A droplet seeped through and clung to the canvas. Another droplet followed, then another and another, until they joined together and trickled down to the dirt floor. Streams ran through the inside of the tent, softening the ground and carving crevices and valleys in the mud. Martha looked down at the river that emerged from beneath her bed. She could see an entire landscape. In a clearing surrounded by thick forest, several tents were grouped together like a colony of mushrooms. She leaned further over the side of the bed and breathed in the smell of damp soil. A girl climbed out of a gully, jumped into the river and swam downstream. She was part of the secret group that lived hidden in the forest.

When Mr. K moved out for the final time, Mrs. K told him to get rid of all the tarpaulin covered mounds he had created in the back garden. She emptied every cupboard, wardrobe and drawer in the house and packed all his belongings into boxes which she then put out on the front lawn. Martha's parents helped to move Mr. K's boxes to the old rundown house he had bought in an adjoining suburb. The house was hidden from the street by a mass of dark green shrubs. Martha and her brother were told to stay in the car while their parents carried boxes from the car to the verandah. Martha sat beside her brother with a small carton on her lap. Inside the carton were a round brown jug and four small cups. They had come from Egypt and had something to do with Mr. K fighting or escaping during the War. Mrs. K had found the jug and cups in the back corner of the top shelf of a tall cupboard in her kitchen. She put them into a carton, handed it to Martha and said she could keep it.

While her parents carried boxes, Martha carefully took out the brown jug and stroked its smooth round belly. She held it up to show her brother. He was not interested in the jug and refused to look at it, but all of a sudden, he looked up and stared past the side of Martha's head. Martha turned and saw Mr. K peering into the car. His face was red and tears streamed down his cheeks. He tapped on the car window. Martha stuffed the jug back into the carton. Mr. K flung his arms onto the roof of the car, buried his head in his arms and sobbed. Martha's parents rushed to the car. Her father led him back to the house. Martha got out of the car to follow them. Her mother ordered her to get back in, then she made sure the back doors were locked and sat in the front passenger seat. A few months later, Martha's family visited Mr. K in the late evening. He opened the door and his bald head and protruding ears seemed huge in the glow of the lamp behind him. He stretched out his arms and leaned forward as if to embrace all four of them. They entered the house and walked through it in single file. There were no floorboards except in the kitchen. Martha walked along a wooden beam like a gymnast, occasionally glancing at the darkness below. Mr. K said it was time for a new beginning. In the kitchen, Martha's mother opened a kitchen cupboard and they all peered through a large hole into the backyard. Mr. K lived in his shell of a house for two years until he had another stroke and died.

Mrs. K's house was dark for much of the day. The constant half-light made every object seem immovable, as if each had grown into its own place and taken root. Martha had tried to raise the venetian blinds, inching it up bit by bit. One half of the blinds jerkily followed the other half then collapsed. She struggled with the looped string, trying to get a rhythm that would draw up the entirety of the blinds, but each time one half reached the halfway point it dropped. After that she let the blinds be. She discovered that the dark and poky bedroom was damp. The small window looked out on a high wooden side fence and tall dark bushes that overshadowed the house. She was glad to have to get up and go to work at the Library, especially since she had temporarily moved to the Manuscripts section. Occasionally she arrived at work very early, more than an hour before any of her colleagues. On those mornings, she liked to walk slowly through the unlit foyer and up the central marble staircase, looking down at the indentations worn into each step. She liked to imagine the ghost of a woman from the early twentieth century walking beside her. Only later, she realised she had conjured Marion Porter before she knew she had existed. The ghost woman walked beside her into the main reading room, and they walked around, looking through the books stacked on the ends of the tables and browsing the shelves. At this time of the morning, Martha was also invisible, as if she had been absorbed into the library and could go anywhere, moving through time unseen.

When she arrived at her usual hour, she often came across her supervisor, Adam Adler. He moved very slowly and deliberately, either going up or down the stairs or walking across the Information Centre. He walked as if he was simultaneously deep in thought and extremely aware of his surroundings. She would slow her pace and they would smile, nodding at each other and saying good morning. From the moment she met him, she thought that Adam Adler looked just like Franz Kafka, although he was shorter and stockier than Kafka had been. Soon after she started at the Library, she learned from a colleague that Adam Adler had come to Australia from Czawa in the 1950s, but no one knew much more than that. Once, they had a brief conversation about a travel writer from Czawa who wrote in English. They discussed his writing style and how it was influenced by his first language; how it was possible to catch glimpses of that prior language inside his writing.

After a few weeks of living in Mrs. K's house, Martha held

a small party. She invited a couple of people from work and a few friends, including Angela who she hadn't seen for a long time. She spent all day preparing food. She made ratatouille and beetroot soup just as her father used to make it. She bought small pastries to go with the soup. The soup was not quite right and the ratatouille was slightly bitter, but she put the food out in Mrs. K's crystal bowls and long serving trays anyway. A few people arrived and soon the place was crowded. Angela arrived with her new boyfriend. A poet from the Library arrived on his own. Tom was supposed to come but had been vague about when he would arrive. Martha filled glasses with wine or vodka and filled her own glass several times. Two more work colleagues arrived, then an actor friend with three other theatre people. Someone turned up the music. Tom did not arrive. The theatre people wanted to dance. A card table was turned over and wine spilled on the carpet. Hela said she would help fix the stain the next day. Martha leaned against the door frame and announced that she was planning a trip. Angela asked where she wanted to go. Martha put one arm out for balance and drew circles in the air with her other hand: Egypt and Morocco and Czawa and Hungary and Russia. The room began to spin.

~

Mrs. K stayed in Czawa two months longer than she planned. Soon after she returned, she became unwell and after several tests she was diagnosed with throat cancer. Her new doctor said the cancer was slow-growing and she could live with it for years, but a couple of months later Mrs. K was in the hospital. The day Martha went to the hospital, her mother was already seated by the bed. Mrs. K, propped up by several white pillows, looked regal. Her hair, no longer dyed blond and stiff with hairspray, was completely white and looked very soft. Martha stood at the foot of the hospital bed like a child, watching and waiting for instructions. Martha's mother helped Mrs. K into her green satin nightgown. When she was seated on the edge of the bed, Mrs. K directed Martha to take the hairbrush out of the drawer beside the bed and Martha slowly and carefully brushed Mrs. K's soft white hair.

Six months after Mrs. K died, Martha and her mother travelled to Czawa to deliver the ashes to Mrs. K's family. Martha had packed the urn in an overnight bag. On the way to the airport, they sat in the back seat of the taxi with the overnight bag between them. Martha's mother spoke to the urn in the bag, letting Mrs. K know they were on the way. When they were finally seated in the plane and the overnight bag was in the overhead compartment, Martha's mother said she could now stop thinking about Mrs. K. She sat silent and gazed out the window. From time to time, she checked the bag at her feet. When the first meal was served, she smiled and thanked the stewardess. Then she examined the small portions of food arranged on the plastic tray before her. She pointed out to Martha that she had received the correct diabetic meal. When Martha received her plastic tray of food, her mother looked across and compared the two meals. Then she looked up and said she didn't know what to expect when she went back to Czawa. Her mother was dead, her father was dead and she hadn't seen her sisters in so long. She wondered if they would recognise her, she wondered if anyone in the family would know who she was. Martha did not answer. She looked down at her own plastic tray. Suddenly her mother announced that she was hungry and that her food looked good. She began to eat as if everything depended on her finishing the food in front of her.

Martha had first gone to Czawa when she was eleven. She watched her mother put their passport and tickets into the special hidden pocket of her large, new handbag. Before the suitcases were loaded into the car, Martha had counted them, and she counted them again while her mother and brother were saying goodbye to her father. She watched the clocks in the airport. She checked that her mother knew the time. She checked how long they had before they needed to get on the plane. When they got off the plane in Singapore, she shadowed her mother as she went from jewellery shop to jewellery shop, making sure she didn't wander out of the airport into the city beyond and get lost so that they wouldn't find their way back in time and the plane would leave, stranding them in this unknown place, neither here nor there. Martha was relieved when they stayed on the plane during the second stopover. As they approached Zurich, the plane was caught in a storm and circled the airport over and over, lurching as if stumbling over rocks. By the time the plane landed, Martha had vomited twice. They transferred to another plane and landed in Czawa sometime later that morning. A crowd of people called and waved as they emerged from the Customs area. Two men dressed in brown suits held red flowers. Martha was told one was her grandfather and the other her uncle, but she was unsure which was which. A crowd had gathered to greet her mother, as though she was a queen or a famous actress. Everyone wanted to kiss her and embrace her and then they turned to Martha and her brother to hug and squeeze them. That was what she remembered; her mother's wavy black hair, red flowers, men in suits, women's smiling faces. Later that afternoon, Martha, who was taller than her grandmother and almost as tall as her grandfather, lay on the sofa bed in the only room in her grandparents' one bedroom apartment. She watched and listened. She knew she was expected to liven up and follow her older cousin, Arek, downstairs to a playground. Instead, she lay on the couch like a gigantic doll taking up too much space. Four-year-old Klara stood and stared at her. Eventually, her other four-year-old cousin, Eva, tugged at Klara's hand and pulled Klara away.

This time, a smaller group greeted Martha and her mother at the airport. An aunt holding a bunch of red flowers rushed up to Martha's mother and hugged her. Martha hitched her overnight bag onto her shoulder and felt the urn dig into her armpit. She smiled and nodded at everyone as they streamed past to greet her mother. Martha felt she ought to hug someone, so she threw her arms around an old man she thought must be an uncle. Only later did she realize it was a taxi driving friend of her great aunt's. Her mother motioned at Martha to follow a man with a beard. "That's your uncle," she whispered. The man had picked up Martha's bags and was heading towards the carpark. Martha tried to catch up to him. A short plump woman called out and put her arm through Martha's arm. It was her mother's youngest sister. Martha smiled at her aunt then looked over her head and saw her mother heading in the other direction surrounded by a small group, everyone laughing and talking.

Martha sat in the back seat and looked out at the vibrant green countryside. Her uncle drove fast and said they would definitely be at Aunt Barbara's house before the others. He said Barbara's husband drove so slowly they would have to wait an hour. All she could think of saying in reply was that the grass and trees were a wonderful vivid green. Her aunt laughed and said spring was the best time in Czawa.

Klara hadn't gone to the airport. When everyone arrived, she came downstairs and stood in the doorway. Martha and her mother sat at a large table, bowls of salad and platters of meat and bread and pickled mushrooms laid before them on an embroidered white cloth. Klara sat beside Martha and smiled. When Martha could eat no more, Klara beckoned and they went upstairs. Klara opened the door to a small room with a narrow bed against the wall, bookshelves and a wardrobe. It had once been Klara's brother's room, but when he left for Ireland it became a kind of storage room. Martha dumped her suitcase on the floor then looked in Klara's room, across her brother's. The room was bare, with only a low bed and bookshelves packed with books and papers and draped with jewellery and scarves. Klara opened the wardrobe in Martha's room, took out a coat and asked if Martha wanted to go out. Martha's head was spinning but she nodded.

"You nod a lot. I saw you nodding all the time downstairs. I'll take you to a place where they serve good coffee." Martha nodded. They got into Uncle Andrew's small rattling car and Klara drove fast over uneven roads to the long pedestrian precinct which had been the focal point of the city since the nineteenth century. Martha knew about this street from her father and from his sisters. In the evenings after work, Aunt Mary, then a young woman, would take her younger sister by the arm and they would promenade along the street meeting friends, talking, all the time walking up and down. Martha was never sure if this had been before the war or after or before and after. Klara stopped the car suddenly in a side street. She jumped out and Martha followed. They went to a cafe with a dark red interior and sat at a table close to the door. The coffee arrived and they stared at one another as they sipped from their cups. Klara spoke first. She said they both had eyebrows after their grandmother. Then she put her chin forward and said the shape of her jaw and mouth was some kind of genetic anomaly, that no one else in the family had that kind of jaw or mouth. Martha looked at Klara's jaw, which Klara seemed to be thrusting out for her to examine. She held a pose that reminded Martha of an ancient African statue. Klara told Martha that she was studying archaeology and that every summer she went on a dig. In a few weeks she would be going north to a place called White Mud. They were investigating burial mounds and stone circles from a culture that had thrived from the first to fifth century AD. They were still trying to work out what caused the upheavals and migrations that dispersed the settlements. Klara smiled. They looked at each other again. Martha described the nineteenth century building that housed the State Library, where she worked. When the building was first built it had also housed a museum. The museum had moved out several years ago, but Martha liked to imagine the invisible collections, the corridors and storage areas within the renovated Library.

Two days later, after they had walked half the length of the five-kilometre pedestrian precinct, Klara took Martha to the old apartment building where her family had lived when she was a child and in which Martha had stayed for three weeks when she was eleven. The entrance was through a gateway that stank of piss. The herringbone paving seemed more even than Martha remembered, and the courtyard seemed smaller. They climbed the steep wooden stairs to the third floor. The door to the apartment was boarded up but they could see inside through a dusty glass panel. There were holes in the walls, exposed wires, piled up boards and dust everywhere. Klara didn't know who owned the place nor what they were going to do with it. She had read somewhere that the adjoining building was scheduled to be demolished. Martha remembered that all the windows were on the left side of the apartment. She had liked to stand at the window in the middle room and look down into the courtyard. Often a group of children played soccer or some other ball game. They ran from one side of the courtyard to the other, kicking the ball. Sometimes, an elderly woman or man called out and the children stopped their game so that the old person could slowly make their way across the courtyard. Martha remembered watching a girl with long brown plaits who never stopped running and who always seemed to be the first to get the ball. It seemed to Martha that she was watching her mother as a young girl.

Martha craned her neck trying to see the window through the dusty glass panel but she couldn't make it out. They went to the window on the landing and Klara sat on the ledge. Her hair, dyed deep red, glowed in the sunlight. Martha stepped back and took a small camera out of her bag. She took a photograph of Klara sitting sideways and looking down into the courtyard. It was the first photograph she had taken of her. That night, Martha awoke and didn't know where she was. She lay still and stared into the darkness. When she closed her eyes again, she found herself at the bottom of a deep and narrow crevice. Smooth black rock glistened on either side. She could hear Klara breathing but when she reached out, she touched nothing.

Sometimes they wandered about in a clearing across the road from the new house that Uncle Andrew had built over many years. They lay in the tall grass and Klara told her that the area had been a military shooting range or ammunition testing site and had only recently been abandoned. She said that from time to time they came across piles of bullets or old shooting targets and some said there were old mines left behind. Martha sat up. "Now lovers mainly come here," Klara smiled. Martha looked around. "I remember that when I was sixteen you were going to come. Everyone was waiting but you never arrived." Martha picked up a stick and scratched the ground with it. She said she had been circling, floating around Europe, not really sure what she was doing. She hadn't finished the advanced French language course but still hung around. She made a few trips to Italy and to Spain. She left Czawa for last, to stay there the longest, but she hadn't left in time.

"That year I moved in with our mothers' cousin, Vera," Klara said. "She lived on her own in an apartment close to my new school. She died two years ago." Martha vaguely remembered a small woman whose hair was always up in a bun and with smiling eyes like a kind grandmother from a fairytale.

"I could do whatever I wanted. She liked to see me have a good time. That's when I met Jacek. Once we got together, we were inseparable. We were like one person. If you had come that year you would have missed me."

"The nuclear accident happened, nobody really knew what was going on and my parents begged me to come back. They said I would be a burden on you all."

"The next year Jacek and I left for the Netherlands."

Martha remembered her mother reading out letters from her sister and shaking her head as she read out that nobody knew exactly where Klara was.

"They knew I was working in a café in Amsterdam, and we came home after a year and a half anyway."

~

Beside her copy of *The Countrysides of Czawa*, Martha kept a copy of a short memoir written by Adam Adler called *No such place*, which was published just after he retired from the Library. The front cover had a picture of Adam wearing a white cap superimposed on a map of Czawa. The book began with an account of his recent trip to Czawa, his first and only trip since he migrated to Australia in 1958. Martha went to the book launch at the Jewish Community Library but arrived late and had to sidestep to a chair in the middle of the back row. After the speeches, she got up awkwardly and made her way to the front of the room to buy the book. She hung back from the group surrounding Adam, but later, finally stepped forward and asked him to sign her copy of the book. He wrote in a large, generous script, 'For Martha, who finally arrived and who is from here but also not from here.' As soon as she got home, she put the book aside to read on the plane. She continued to read it when she arrived in Czawa.

When Adam arrived in Czawa with his wife, he tried to find the apartment he had lived in for the first three years of his life. He spent a day circling the nearby streets and then standing outside the building and looking up at the window. Finally, he entered the apartment building, went to the door and pushed the doorbell beside it. An elderly man opened the door and Adam began his prepared speech. He assured the man he did not want to trouble him but that he had lived in the apartment before the war until the age of three and wondered if he could spend just a few minutes looking around the place he had loved so much. The old man said his family had been allocated the flat after the war and that he'd been living there with his wife and parents ever since. He opened the door wider and Adam entered. As they walked around the apartment, the old man explained that his parents had died, and now he and his wife lived in the flat and occasionally looked after their grandson. Adam said very little. Most of his memories of the place were somehow entwined with his mother. They stopped before an alcove with bookshelves. Adam recognised a book of children's poems. He took the book off the shelves and opened it. The man stood beside him as he turned the pages.

In 1943, when Adam was seven years old, he was given a false name and had gone into hiding. His mother could only visit him rarely. She had a forged identification card and would show it to him to remind him of her assumed name. The apartment in which he was hiding was on the third and top floor of a large block. He spent his time between one of the two rooms in the apartment and the roof space above. He was never allowed near the windows which looked down onto the courtyard. He became used to avoiding windows during the day and turned into the room. One wall was covered with bookshelves from floor to ceiling and there were more books on lower shelves on another wall. He slept on a folding sofa bed. The apartment had belonged to a writer and well-known activist. When she was arrested and taken away, her nieces moved in. At lunchtime, paying guests arrived at the apartment to eat their meals. This was how the two sisters made enough money to live.

The seven-year-old boy spent the mornings reading. He chose books at random, by book cover or size. He did not know it then, but he had access to a great library of literature from classics to modern fiction and translations in many languages. Just before customers arrived for the mid-day meal, one of the sisters would put a chair on the table. The boy climbed onto the chair then pulled himself up through a little trap door into the roof space above. It was completely dark except for some light coming from small cracks between the roof tiles. There was a blanket and some pillows, and he would sit or lie there until he heard the all clear signal of three taps on the kitchen ceiling. While he lay in the dark, he whispered the names of all the publishers of the books he had read. In this way, he conjured up the books, the first page with the publisher's emblem and its particular typeface and put it aside, as if to save for later.

When Martha first read the memoir, she read quickly. It had a large print, the lines were well spaced and it was made up of episodes as if not to waste time. She reread the section about Adam's mother's childhood twice. It was a story hinting that Adam's mother, Ada, had run into Franz Kafka when she was a young girl. Just before the outbreak of the First World War,

Ada's family had temporarily moved to Prague and she had gone to a school for foreign children. She worked out a route to the school through the narrow and winding streets of the old town and kept to it every day. Along this route she would pass a shiny blue-grey cobblestone. It was slightly raised, rounded and worn very smooth by the many feet that had stepped on it. Every day on her way to and from school, she made sure to step on it for good luck, but one afternoon on her way home she forgot. During school that day, she had put up her hand and answered the teacher's question about a poem she had read for the first time in a language that was new to her. She did it without thinking. No one else in the class had raised their hand and it was the first time she had spoken in class. The teacher nodded and asked her to repeat what she had said so that everyone could hear and understand. When she passed the cobblestone, Ada was thinking of the moment she put up her hand. As soon as she realized she had forgotten to step on the stone, she whirled around and her school bag flew out of her hand. It landed on the footpath and nearly everything inside fell out; books, pencils, rulers lay scattered over the footpath. A tall dark-haired man approached and asked if she was lost. Ada shook her head and said she had just forgotten something and when she remembered it, she had dropped her bag. They both crouched and picked up Ada's things. The man looked at the cover of one of her notebooks and asked if the A stood for Anna. "No, my name is Ada. I don't come from here." The man nodded and introduced himself as Franz and said he was both from this place and not from this place. Ada didn't know what to say but somehow, he mentioned that he worked in an insurance office and also wrote stories. Ada wanted to know about the stories and the man said he hoped she would read them one day when she grew up. She thanked him again and went on her way. She never saw him again. Years later, when she worked in a publishing house in Czawa, she came across a translation of the letters of Kafka and wondered if the man she had bumped into was the writer. Martha had no doubt that the man was Franz Kafka and that his shadow somehow flitted across or through Adam Adler's face whenever she met him on the marble staircase in the State Library.

~

Every day and nearly every night for a week, Klara and Martha went out. During the day, they sometimes went to a museum or gallery, but they mainly wandered the streets, sauntering with their arms linked. Klara pointed out the old apartment buildings that she liked, the dirty facades, the gateways with peeling paint, the faded, sometimes crumbling window casements. She liked that the exteriors of the buildings had aged and become decrepit, that no one had restored them. One afternoon on their way home, they passed a small shoe shop. Klara stopped and pointed at a pair of tall boots in the window. "You could go anywhere in boots like that," she said. Martha gazed at the strong, well-made boots. The brown leather gleamed. Klara said she had been eyeing them for weeks, she had tried them on and they fit perfectly but they were too expensive. Martha continued to stare into the shop window; she could go into the shop and buy the boots for Klara then and there. She hesitated. She didn't want to make any grand gestures, since she didn't know what was expected or how it would be taken. Klara suggested Martha buy the boots for herself. Martha tilted her head as if thinking about it, but she had already made up her mind. The boots were for Klara. She would buy them as a surprise present just before she left and then, whenever Klara put on the boots, she would be reminded of Martha. She would take Martha with her on her trips into the countryside, on her travels through towns and cities.

That evening they went to a nightclub. Martha wore one of Klara's favourite dresses. It was long and black and a little too loose. The club was already crowded when they arrived. Someone waved to Klara and Martha followed her to a table where three young men sat drinking. Klara knew one of them from the University. The men joked and talked fast. Martha struggled to keep up with the conversation. She tried to describe where she lived in Melbourne, where she worked, but words ran out and she became so tired she could hardly open her mouth. Klara's friend said he wanted to practice English. He was drunk and declaimed over and over as if jabbing her with his finger:

> *a pair of glasses*
>
> *two pairs of jeans*
>
> *the city of London*
>
> *Where do you go after work?*

Klara had her back to Martha and was talking and laughing with a tall, thin man seated beside her. Martha gazed around the room then looked down at her shoes. Eventually, they all left the nightclub and walked to a new place. They walked fast and Martha soon fell behind. The tall thin man slowed his pace to walk beside her. When they reached the next bar, he bought Martha a drink and sat beside her. He hunched over as if to shield her from the noise and with a half-smile looked at her, waiting for her to speak. Martha examined his long straight nose and high cheekbones and remained silent.

~

After nearly two years away with her old boyfriend, mostly working in a cafe in Amsterdam but also travelling in Turkey and Greece, Klara had returned to Czawa and decided to study archaeology. She told Martha that it was the only thing that interested her. They sat on the floor in Klara's room sipping tea.

Klara put down her cup and fetched a large book from the low bookcase beside her bed. She opened the archaeological text to a chapter on the ancient Roman town of Herculaneum. She clasped her knees close to her chest. Martha edged closer so that they sat side by side before the open book. Martha knew little about Herculaneum and listened to Klara describe the eruption of Vesuvius, how the entire town had been buried in a flowing mixture of ash and hot gasses and remained preserved for nearly nineteen centuries. Almost everything that had been blanketed in hot ash remained intact. Bowls of food stood on the tables where they had been left and even the food in the bowls was preserved. The people that had been eating from those bowls fled but were killed just moments after they left the house. In Pompeii, the bodies of entire families were found trying to protect themselves and each other; mothers curled around children and fathers stood in the doorways as if to keep guard. Martha peered at the plaster cast of a dog chained to a post, curled around it as if asleep; an animal turned to stone. Klara turned the page. Archaeologists had still not excavated the whole of Herculaneum because a new town, Resina, had been built on top of the buried city. Klara flicked through the book and pointed to a photograph. A rundown but modern apartment building stood at one end of a street that dropped away and beneath it, in what looked like a hollow, was the entrance to a large room. Just a few metres beneath the buildings of Resina lay the ancient streets and buildings of Herculaneum. Large sections of Herculaneum were waiting to be excavated but all the people living in the town on top would have to be moved out. She flicked through the book again until she found a photograph of a section of Herculaneum that was open to the sky. Behind a few uncovered rooms in buildings on an ancient street, was a wall of rock and earth that had been excavated. Perched on top of this wall, as if on the edge of a cliff or ravine, were several blocks of flats. Martha took the book from Klara and peered at the white sheets and clothes hanging on a washing line suspended between two of the modern buildings. She wanted to see, but couldn't, where the washing line came from and how it was attached. She passed the book back to Klara expecting her to find another photograph. Klara put the book aside and pointed at the ring on Martha's right middle finger. She had never seen an amethyst such a rich purple. Martha held out her hand as if offering it to be kissed. Klara held Martha's fingers lightly and peered at the ring. Then she looked up and said she could see a light deep inside the stone. Martha took off the ring Mrs. K had left her so that Klara could examine it. The ring was old, and Martha thought it had been handed down through several generations. It had probably come from Vilnius. Klara didn't know anything about Mrs. K. Martha explained that when her mother first arrived in Melbourne, Mrs. K had taken her mother under her wing. She and her husband showed Martha's mother the city of Melbourne. Martha knew that Mrs. K had met Mr. K when he was studying at the University, and that they were determined to marry even though Mrs. K's family objected for reasons to do with class. Almost as soon as they married, however, they were separated. In the first days of the war, Mr. K was captured and put on a train with other captured officers, heading for an isolated forest where they were to be executed. Mr. K threw himself off the train, escaped and made his way to Persia. Mrs. K escaped deportation and joined a group of women and children heading west. She carried her belongings in a large bag and all her jewellery, except for the amethyst ring, was hidden in her underclothes. She wore the ring on her finger with the stone turned in towards her palm. As the women and children trudged through a field, they heard, then saw, planes flying low towards them. They all rushed to the nearest ditch, barely a dip in the flat landscape, and threw themselves into it headfirst. Mrs. K lay there with her eyes closed. She thought of all the women with their faces in the ground, their arms around their heads, their children under their bellies and their bums in the air. She began to laugh. It was an uncontrollable laughter that shook her body and overtook the sound of strafing.

After the war, Mr. K ended up in England, where he got a job as a chauffeur for a rich English woman who lived alone in a large country house not far from London. The rich English woman agreed to employ Mrs. K as a maid. Mrs. K sold nearly everything she had to pay for her escape from Czawa to England. One of the things she didn't sell was the amethyst ring. Early one morning, she was smuggled out of the country beneath a false floor on a fishing boat. Before the boat left the port, she lay flat on her back in the dark holding her breath, listening to the planks above creak beneath the heavy steps of the inspectors' boots. When the inspectors finally got off the boat, she breathed in the stink of old herring and kept her eyes closed all the way to Sweden.

Two days before Martha and her mother were going to stay with Mrs. K's relatives, Klara took Martha to the only remaining Jewish cemetery in Nadwodom. She told Martha that the cemetery was known as the New Jewish cemetery and founded in 1892. The Old cemetery, on the edge of the Old Town, had been destroyed during the war and a new street with housing was built on the grounds in the 1950s.

The cemetery seemed huge to Martha. There were over a hundred thousand marked graves and a field commemorating victims from the Ghetto who had died of hunger and consumption. The further they walked away from the grand front gates, the wilder the place became. Parts of the cemetery were like a forest glade, with birch trees and lindens and greenish engraved headstones emerging from the undergrowth. Other parts of the cemetery were like fields, with wildflowers and grasses. Some decorated tombs and headstones teetered to one side, much of their engraved garlands, fruit and animals worn away while others seemed to have been restored. Klara and Martha stood before a headstone, half-sunk into the ground, decorated with birds and baskets of fruit. The Hebrew lettering engraved on the stone looked ancient and mysterious. Martha wanted to run her fingers over the unknown words as if touching them would make them understandable or would bring back the people who would have mourned the dead person, the people who would have understood the inscription, the people who could have explained the inscription.

Klara and Martha hadn't spoken much since they entered the cemetery. Now, staring at the dilapidated headstone, Klara said that Martha ought to stay longer, that there was hardly any time to do anything. Martha said that maybe she could, that she wanted to stay longer and wanted to see more. She wanted to travel with Klara, but she couldn't really see how. Klara smiled then turned and ran through the long grass. Martha stood and watched as Klara ran, getting further and further away, becoming smaller until all that she could see was her dyed red hair and a bit of her long, indigo dress. Martha took out her camera and photographed all that was visible of Klara.

When they returned, Martha went to her room to pack for the trip. Klara followed and sat on the end of the bed. Her long, indigo coloured dress was made of very light material. Martha touched the hem then held the material in her hand and let it slip off her fingers. She would have liked a dress exactly the same. Klara said she would look out for one when she returned to the city. She was leaving to work on an archaeological site near a village called White Mud in two days' time. Martha took clothes from her suitcase and put them into an overnight bag. The archaeological site was on the edge of a lake. The ancient objects found there, pottery and jewellery and even birch-bark fishing floats, had been submerged in water and mud for a thousand years, preserved and kept safe in the marshes.

Early the next morning, Martha, her mother and uncle left for the village where Mrs. K's family lived. Her mother had taken possession of the urn containing Mrs. K's ashes and had an envelope of money to deliver. Martha sat in the back seat of the car and listened to her mother chatting with her uncle. Martha's mother had developed a nervous way of sucking in air at the end of each sentence, as if she had a sore tooth. Martha had noticed this soon after they arrived in Czawa, but it seemed to have become worse in the confined space of the car. Every now and again she thought of saying something, but she shut her mouth and gazed out the window. As they approached the village, her uncle pointed out examples of typical farmhouses in the region, wooden buildings that combined house and barn, with roofs of wooden shingles. Martha stared at the low buildings with small windows. Her mother sucked in air without saying anything and her uncle explained that when the borders were redrawn, the German inhabitants of the farmhouses had to move west and the people displaced from Eastern Czawa moved into the vacated houses, into buildings that were quite foreign to them.

At night, Martha and Anna lay in separate beds on either side of the room. They both stared into the dark. There was a strong smell of sour milk. The smell made Anna nauseous and it was all she could do to stop herself from retching.

"This is why I could never live in the country," she whispered. "I don't know why they put us in the room where they make yoghurt and cheese. All those pots on the ledges and around the room are full of sour milk. We're surrounded."

Martha supposed it was because they had nowhere else to put them. "Anyway, the funeral service or whatever it is, is tomorrow isn't it? Then we can go."

"We can't just go. We have to meet the rest of the family. After that Barbara and Andrew will come to collect us and we'll go north to stay with my cousin for a few days."

"Since when did you organise this?" Martha hissed. "Klara is waiting for me at the archaeological camp near White Mud."

"What do you want to go there for?" Anna couldn't understand why anyone would want to dig in mud, surrounded by nothing but empty marshland and exposed to ticks.

They lay in silence.

Then Anna said, "I once wanted to be an archaeologist, but I couldn't draw and you had to be able to draw. In a way it's funny that my niece, who hardly knows me, is an archaeologist, or so she says."

Martha sighed.

For a few days, it had seemed possible for her to get on the train that stopped at the village of White Mud and arrive in the early evening, possible for Klara to be waiting for her. She had imagined that they would walk through the forest in the half-light, following a narrow, sandy track past a lake surrounded by reeds, to the small wooden cabin where Klara was staying. Somehow, without her realising it, she had been hijacked.

Martha's mother half-sat up and adjusted her bedding. She said that just before they left Melbourne, she had a dream where she saw Martha's face very close. She wanted to stroke Martha's cheek, but her face moved away. The more she tried to reach it, the further Martha's face moved away, until it floated high like the moon. It wasn't good to see a face floating like that. She thought it might have been some kind of warning. She told Martha that she had had one strange dream after another. Just a week ago, she dreamed that she was rushing along a crowded street carrying a tiny baby bundled up in a blanket. People blocked her way, and she couldn't get through. Even the road was blocked. Cars were at a standstill. She ran between the cars and eventually got to the other side. She stood in the middle of the pavement and looked around. She didn't know which way to go, she didn't know this street, this place. As if from a distance, she saw herself turning this way and that and then she bumped into a man and dropped the baby. She froze. She watched a shopkeeper run out from a doorway, pick up the baby and carry it into a shop. She ran into the shop but it was too late. The shop was deserted.

Martha listened to her mother turn in her bed again and pat her pillow. She assured her mother that she wouldn't abandon her or disappoint Mrs. K's relatives. While Klara and the group of archaeologists carefully uncovered utensils, jewellery, small sculptures and bones from deep in the soft grey mud surrounding the lake, while they pieced together a history of the ancient people that had once lived there from these fragments, she would be sitting at a table covered with an embroidered tablecloth and smiling at one of Mrs. K's elderly relatives and the local priest.

Over the next four days, Martha and her mother tried the various cheeses they made in the farmhouse, wandered around the farmyard, met visitors and ate specially prepared dinners. It turned out that the priest liked to joke and became quite boisterous after a couple shots of vodka. He sat at the table beside

Martha. Her mother sat on her other side beside Mrs. K's elderly cousin. She spoke in a soft, rounded accent that Martha's mother explained was how they spoke in the far eastern provinces of Czawa. The elderly cousin wore a black dress and kept one hand on Martha's mother's arm and the other gripping the table as if to anchor them both. She wanted to know all about their life in Australia and their friendship with Mrs. K. She observed Martha's mother as she spoke, observed all her movements. Then she announced that she had never met anyone from Nadwodom, "Red Nadwodom, the city of reds and unrest." She laughed and patted Anna on the arm. The priest guffawed, "Altogether a dangerous place they tell me." He winked and nudged Martha.

Early on the morning of the fifth day, Andrew and Barbara drove them north to the sea and to the port city where Martha's mother had a favourite cousin. Klara had insisted that they call in to White Mud on the way. Uncle Andrew drove slowly as though to stretch out time. Cars and trucks rushed past them. Martha looked at her watch then rested her cheek against the window and closed her eyes. Three weeks ago, when she and Klara had spent two days in the oldest city in Czawa, she had sat on a bench in the market square facing the sun. Klara went to buy tickets to a play. Martha waited half-asleep in the warm sun and then through half-closed eyes, saw a woman approach. For a moment, Martha thought it had been her mother. The woman wore big skirts and a scarf around her head. She held out her hand as she walked towards Martha. Martha shifted along the bench as if about to get up but stayed seated. The woman stood before her with an outstretched hand and said something Martha couldn't understand. Martha looked away, then felt in her pocket and without looking at the woman, gave her a couple of coins. As the woman left, Martha noticed an almost translucent, smooth, grey stone wedged in the cobblestones where the woman had stood. She picked up the stone and ran her thumb over it. It was round and hard, like a hard boiled lolly. She put it in her pocket and ran her fingers over it from time to time.

Anna nudged Martha and asked why she was so quiet, and was she unwell? Without waiting for an answer, Anna said it was stuffy in the car and asked Martha to open the window on her side just a little so there wouldn't be any draught. Martha opened the window wide then slowly turned the handle back up so that there was only a crack letting in air. Anna told her sister and brother-in law that when Martha was four, she didn't speak for days. She thought something must have happened, but she had no idea what. She wrote a letter to their mother to get some advice. There was no reply for months. She said Barbara should have let her know that their mother was sick and in hospital straight away. Aunt Barbara said they were all so busy when their mother got sick, she hardly had time to go and buy food. They were constantly in and out of the hospital, bringing food and looking out for the doctor and nurses. Anna made a sucking noise. Martha took the smooth grey stone out of her pocket and pressed it against her temple.

They arrived at the archaeological base just after 1p.m.. The place seemed deserted. Aunt Barbara wandered ahead calling out and eventually Klara emerged from a small wooden cabin. She rushed over to Martha and they hugged as if they hadn't seen each other for years. Klara led them to a wooden hall and then went to the kitchen to make tea. They sat at a long table by the open door with a view of the main entrance. There was no one in sight. Klara returned with tea and cups and Aunt Barbara laid out the bread, ham and cheese she had brought with her. Klara explained that more students and workers and researchers were due to arrive the next day. She said the lake was just a short walk through the trees and after they had finished eating and drinking, they could walk to the lake and go out in a row boat. Martha's mother didn't think they had enough time. Aunt Barbara looked as if she would have liked to go out on the lake and so did Uncle Andrew, but they agreed it would be better to leave earlier. They drank more tea. Klara looked in the direction of the trees and said that even though it was the third time she had been at this site she could never get enough of the place. She felt like a different person. Then she laughed and said that she actually would have liked the name Renata instead of Klara. In fact, from time to time she introduced herself as Renata. Anna raised her eyebrows and said she thought the name Klara was perfectly fine. She looked at her watch and said she hoped they wouldn't arrive at her cousin's place too late.

Martha looked at Klara, "Let's go for a walk. Come on Renata, show me around."

Klara linked her arm through Martha's and led her to the shore of the lake. Martha was expecting to see some evidence of the dig, perhaps some recently excavated artifacts. She asked Klara why the place was so quiet. Klara said that people came and went and that she liked spending time there on her own, lying around and reading, before all the others arrived. They walked further around the lake. Neither of them spoke. Martha savoured walking on the uneven ground and listened to the crunch of small pebbles beneath her feet. Around a bend, they saw an old manor house painted yellow with a large pillar on either side of the porch. Klara said that an artist had bought the place a couple of years ago and spent every summer there. They walked to the manor house and stood on the porch. Klara winked at Martha and called through the open door, "It's Renata here with her sister." A man's voice called out to them to come in. They walked through the dark entrance and came to a large, almost bare room. A man stood at a very big wooden table looking through a pile of drawings. A dark-haired woman was taking photographs of drawings arranged on another table. She looked up as they entered. The artist kept shuffling and examining the drawings with one hand and said he had to choose material for an exhibition. He sighed and stepped back, then with a sweep of his arm invited them to take a look. The pictures had been drawn or painted in black on large sheets of white paper. They were mainly portraits, strange portraits of the same sad looking man, sometimes of a woman painted in the same style – expressive unrealistic outlines of heads and shoulders in strong lines. The artist's companion moved away from the table and went to a large leather chest that stood against the wall of the almost empty room. She carefully packed the drawings she had been photographing into the leather chest. Klara and the artist discussed the pictures. Martha nodded. There were dozens and dozens of drawings and paintings. She wanted to see them all. When the pictures were packed away, she looked around at the worn wooden parquet floor and then at the leather chest by the wall. She wondered what the rest of the house looked like, whether all the rooms were so bare and sparse, so full of moving shadows.

They all walked to the edge of the lake, Klara and the artist talking all the while. Martha looked at her watch. She could feel her mother's impatience. When they reached the lake, they stood among the reeds and looked out at the blue grey water in silence. All around them there was a slight tremor, as if the landscape was shaking.

They returned to the manor house and the artist's companion disappeared into another room to prepare something to eat. The artist didn't seem to notice. Martha watched her go out; to prepare and provide food must have been one of her jobs. She returned, carrying a tray with a plate of dark bread and pickles, some small glasses and a bottle of vodka. They emptied the small glasses of vodka and ate the small squares of dark bread and pickle. Then the artist turned to Martha, "Renata says you're going to write something, so what are you going to write?" The artist's companion looked at her with her head to one side. Martha looked at Klara. The artist said Martha should write something about Czawa. Martha looked at a small square of dark bread that was the colour of chocolate. She remembered a scene in a play she had seen years ago. It was the only scene she remembered and in her mind it had become a whole new play. A woman stood on a stage surrounded by objects invisible to the audience. The woman had collected the objects that were piled up around her but now kept her captive. She told stories about how every now and again she escaped these objects from her past but then she always returned with yet another object.

Before they left, the artist's companion laid out four pictures, all portraits, on the side table. She asked each of them which picture they preferred. Klara pointed at a portrait painted in black ink, with dark pools for eyes, and thick lines delineating the head then dissolving into trickles. Martha could not decide which picture she liked best. The artist pushed forward a portrait; a series of outlines of a woman's head which gave the impression of constant movement. He said that was the picture for Martha, then carefully rolled up each picture.

~

Klara told Martha she would write letters. She said she hardly ever wrote letters and took ages to write them, but she would write Martha long letters that would arrive when Martha least expected it. All in all, Klara wrote three letters to Martha after the trip to deliver Mrs. K's ashes. Martha kept them in a purple folder. When each letter first arrived, she read it over several times then filed it away in the folder.

The first and longest letter arrived a few weeks after Martha returned to Melbourne. Klara wrote that she had stayed at the dig for some time after Martha left. 'We discovered three burial sites pre-AD 150. They contained urns with human ashes, a few bronze pins and a bronze belt buckle. The belt buckle was an important find since few of them have been found in Central Europe from this era. Each urn and the objects with it were surrounded by large, beautiful stones as if they were packed in specially selected stones for protection.' Klara described the heat and how they regularly stopped to drink beer, which made the work go easily. In the evenings they went to a tavern, more than a hundred years old, in the local village. 'Imagine walls with peeling paint, rickety tables, drunk peasants (although not aggressive, in fact rather gracious), dirty glasses and crap folk music. The walls are painted green and the lamps have an orange glow which gives everyone a corpse-like look. It sounds terrible but there is something that draws you in to this other world. I think you need to experience something like this and maybe you'd write about it.'

'On the way back from the tavern, we walked two kilometres through a completely dark forest. It would've been fine if the moon was out, but that night there was no moonlight so we groped our way through, as if blindfolded, and only made it back to the base because we had developed a sort of body memory.'

In the second letter, Klara wrote that Norbert came to visit with his friend Kris. 'Of course, you know Norbert, and you know Kris, he was the tall thin one you talked to at the nightclub that we went to soon after you arrived (don't get him mixed up with Peter who spoke in English the whole time). We met up a few times and Kris and I have started a pleasant affair which is going to this day although I plan to call it off soon.'

The third letter arrived many months later. 'I'm still working on my thesis to do with early medieval settlements. I've run into a bit of trouble – will write about it another time. It's a pity you're not here now. It's wonderful weather for taking photographs. The light is grey-black yet very sharp and clear. The buildings seem completely different and the streets are transformed, suddenly narrow then opening out when you least expect it, even people's faces are distorted. When I walk, I sometimes lose sense of my body so that I'm like an observing eye and nothing else floating above the passersby who walk with their heads lowered. This will all end once it begins to snow but now it is really unsettling.'

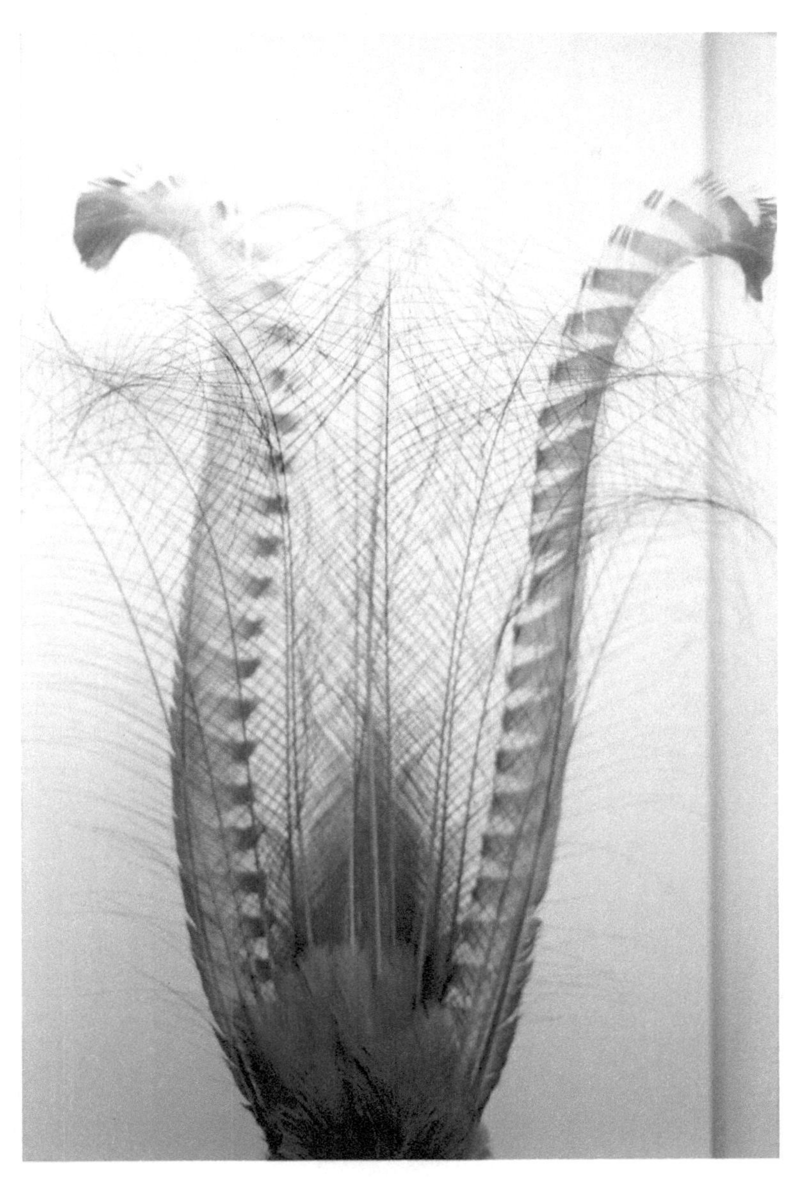

III

GIRL AT THE WINDOW

On the floor by her bed, Martha had a 'Travel to Czawa' pile of guidebooks and a notebook. Three years after her last trip, she finally had enough time and money to go to Czawa again and to stay for just over a month. She collected information from guidebooks and general surveys as if she had never been to Nadwodom, never been to Czawa, as if she was an English-speaking tourist with a general interest in those places or as if she only had some kind of loose connection to the place. She read the historical summaries closely and made notes, lightly marking the outer edges of the city, observing it from the outside. Nearly everything she read in these guides began with a paragraph about the population of Nadwodom in the nineteenth century before the war, a kind of introduction to what would be lost. In the nineteenth century, the small town of weavers grew at a great pace into a large industrial city and became the centre of a huge textile industry. The population of this far-flung industrial capital belonging to the Russian empire came from the nearby countryside, from regions further away and from other countries. The industrialists built palaces, more factories and workers' housing close to the factories. The factory complexes included schools, hospitals, fire brigades, workers' housing, and the factory owner's residence. Theatres, cafes and hotels sprang up in other parts of the city. By the end of the nineteenth century, the city was like a huge, noisy, fast-paced weaving machine. During the Second World War, under the German occupation, the Jewish population of Nadwodom was forced into a Ghetto and large numbers of people were periodically sent to extermination camps. By the end of the war, the city's population which had consisted of people from several different cultures and religions was destroyed.

Martha first came across Marion Porter a couple of months before she arranged her trip. She was almost at the end of her six-month stint in the Manuscripts Collection at the State Library. Marion Porter had died many years earlier and a relative had finally sent her papers and photographs to the Library. Eight boxes were brought up to the Manuscripts section. All the photographs went to the Picture Collection and all the papers stayed in Manuscripts. Martha helped unpack the boxes and volunteered to do an initial listing of their contents. One afternoon, she flicked through one of the diaries that Marion Porter had kept intermittently. She noticed a relatively long entry for April 6th, 1970. Marion wrote that she had finally started to paint the palings of her front fence. While she painted, a ruddy faced man stopped and stood on the pavement beside her. He watched for a moment then commented on the pale blue colour of the paint. He had a strong accent but spoke English well. She asked if he was new to the area. He said that years ago, he had lived in a house a few streets away before he left Australia to go back to Czawa. He had spent several years in Czawa but now he was back and was looking for somewhere to live. He walked away with a slight limp, looking at each house he passed as if assessing whether it would be a suitable place to live. Marion was curious about the man and what he was really doing wandering around the streets. She wrote that she would keep an eye out in case he showed up again. Martha skimmed the rest of the diary looking for another mention of the ruddy faced man, but he never reappeared. On the back page of her own notebook, Martha wrote: Mr. K stood with his hands in his pockets and watched an old woman with grey-brown hair painting a wooden fence without pause, as if he wasn't there.

~

At the far end of the almost empty platform Klara walked quickly towards the train. Martha leaned out the carriage window and waved then dragged her suitcase down the corridor and bumped it onto the platform. They approached each other waving and calling, not quite sure how to look at each other. When they were close, they hugged and kissed, then Klara explained that the station was being renovated and most trains were being shunted elsewhere. Martha remembered how fast Klara talked, how she jumped from one topic to another. They talked all that day and into the night until Martha could no longer keep her eyes open.

Klara lived in the top section of a two-storey house in a suburb that bordered the forest reserve to the east of the city. She had renovated the upstairs section so that it included a kitchen and bathroom and a studio or lounge room. She insisted that Martha stay in her bedroom and she slept on a large foldout sofa in the lounge room. First thing in the morning, Martha stood before Klara's tall bedroom window and looked down at the small green back garden with the sheds bordering the forest reserve. Then she put her hands on the wide windowsill which was more like a ledge. The window was framed by long, diaphanous rose coloured curtains that hung from metal black rods. She looked out at the treetops over the sheds and breathed in green and light.

She sat at the kitchen table while Klara made coffee and already knew it would be a sunny day. She asked Klara what the sheds were for. Klara said they had once been used as motorbike sheds. People who had no space in the city would rent the sheds and even though it didn't make sense for them to keep their bikes so far away, that was what the authorities had allowed. Now, she just kept her bicycle and a motor scooter that needed fixing in one of the sheds. Her old boyfriend still had his bike in there too so they could ride into the city together later on. Martha wondered what had happened to the old boyfriend. Just a couple of months ago, she had called Klara and a boyish, slightly gaunt man with large brown eyes appeared on the computer screen. He nodded, said hello and then all she saw was his red tee-shirt as he wobbled the laptop over to Klara who was giggling in the background. Klara said she didn't like having him around all the time; they weren't suited and there was too much arguing.

During her first trip to Nadwodom, when she was eleven, Martha considered the apartment where her aunt had lived with her family to be the centre of the city and she still thought of it that way. The apartment was on the top floor of a three-storey tenement, built at the end of the nineteenth century and just off the main pedestrian thoroughfare. It seemed to Martha that the narrow, cobbled courtyard, the staircase, the various apartments within the building, contained the entire city. The gateway off the street leading to the narrow courtyard, was the entrance to an invisible world, made up of several epochs or periods all laid on top of each other and then folded together.

Martha and her brother followed their mother and aunt into a gateway off the pedestrian promenade. The two sisters walked arm in arm, talking continuously without looking back. They crossed the courtyard then climbed the worn wooden stairs to the third floor. All four entered the apartment together. To the right of the entry hall was a small kitchen with a stove, sink and pantry, and beside it, an alcove just big enough for the washing machine. The entry hall led to the next room which led to another long room which led to the last room. The ceilings were high and the tall windows were all on the left. Over the next few days, Martha found her place standing at the middle window in the middle room looking down at the courtyard or over at the neighbouring apartments. On the mornings she stood with her back to the room, she was nothing but eyes looking down at the paved courtyard and ears listening to the chink of glass teacups and the voices of her mother and aunt.

One morning, Martha stood at the window while her mother and aunt discussed what it was like to live in Nadwodom. Six-year-old Klara and her friend walked around the edge of the courtyard, staying close to the building. Klara's friend had plaits and was nursing a doll. She gave the doll to Klara and watched as Klara sat the doll on a step. Then she followed Klara to a tap on the other side of the courtyard.

Martha's mother and aunt spoke very softly. They discussed whether it would be possible for Martha's mother to live in Czawa.

Klara turned on the tap and crouched before the river forming between the paving stones.

Martha heard her father's name in the hushed stream of words behind her.

A puddle formed near the flowing tap and Klara floated the doll on her back.

Martha stood at the window as thin and transparent as a gauze curtain.

The glass teacups clinked against glass saucers. Martha's brother played soccer with the children in the courtyard below.

The washing machine in the alcove near the entrance rattled and shook. It filled with water and, while no one was watching, overflowed. Water trickled down the side of the washing machine, formed a pool, spread under the door and then flowed down the stairs to the floors below until it reached the front door and spilled out the building.

Klara placed a cup of strong coffee in front of Martha and pushed forward a tray of strawberries. "Just before you arrived, my mother dreamed that she was at your mother's wedding. She didn't want to wake up." Martha smiled. Her parents hadn't had a proper wedding. They met at a party when her mother was nineteen and her father was thirty. Anna arrived on her Jawa motorcycle with a boyfriend riding pillion. She was introduced to Martha's father and the boyfriend left the party early. Martha's father already had all the documents he needed to migrate to Australia. Six months after the party, her parents were engaged, and it was inevitable that Anna would leave Czawa. Martha had seen a photograph taken at the engagement party. Her father was wearing a beret, holding a cigarette in his hand and smiling at his future wife who had taken the photo. A couple of weeks later, he sailed to Australia on a ship with his two older sisters and mother. Some months later there was a marriage by proxy and a year later, when Anna had acquired the documents she needed to migrate, Martha's father sent the money for her to make the trip to Australia.

On most evenings of the first week, Martha stayed with Klara. They walked arm in arm, up and down the main pedestrian thoroughfare, looking into cafes and bars. From time to time, when talking had exhausted them both, they walked in silence. One evening when they got home and Martha was more tired than usual, they got ready for bed and reclined on the sofa bed propped up by Klara's pillows. Klara balanced her laptop on her knees and pounded the keyboard as she talked. When she found a video she was looking for, she placed the laptop on the blanket covering their legs so that they could both see the screen. They watched a performance by four male actors. Martha struggled to keep her eyes open while four men on a bare stage with only chairs for props struggled with words and phrases. What they wanted to say drove them into contortions and acrobatics. They shouted at each other then whispered into each other's ears. The sounds coming from their mouths were so powerful that anyone of them could've been turned inside out. Finally, the tallest, most nimble of the actors stood on his head, his body perfectly straight and rigid. A moment later, he crumpled onto the floor. Klara played another episode. One of the men confided to the other, "M-m-mya, myast, litera h, ha hey hoy... oj it's diff, diffi, excuse me, excuse me, may I come in because, excuse me, this is what, what I said to him, this was, was this, what I said to him, and so, what do you think, eh? What do you think?" Then the words fell away. Martha could no longer keep her eyes open or her head up. She fell asleep slumped against the pillow, her head resting on Klara's shoulder.

When she awoke, she could see a dim light coming from the kitchen. Klara slept beside her and the laptop had disappeared. They were both under a huge white feather doona big enough to block out the world. Martha touched the gold red strands of Klara's hair spread on the edge of her pillow. She remembered her grandparents calling her to their bed when she stayed, together with her mother and little brother, in their tiny flat in Malin, a town outside Nadwodom. She would get into the bed and lie between them under the biggest, whitest doona she had ever seen. One morning when her cousins were also staying in the tiny flat, they all climbed into the bed. Martha, her brother, Klara and Eva were all underneath the white doona, which was like a sweet, musty-smelling cocoon. Martha lay still, breathing in the warm fur-like smell and occasionally touching the white stiff cotton doona cover, but then the white doona heaved. Sections collapsed, others billowed. Her brother and cousins wriggled and squirmed, their feet, legs and arms colliding. She burst out from the bedclothes afraid of being smothered, then stood by the bed gazing down at them. Her grandfather laughed, her cousins giggled, but her grandmother turned her head on the huge white pillow and looked at her without smiling.

On a grey, windy day, Klara took her on a tour of the city's original sewerage tunnels which had just been opened as a kind of museum. As they walked through the tunnels, Klara explained that seven small rivers had been covered over many years ago and now ran underground beneath the streets in a system of canals. She said the drinking water from these small rivers was the best in all Czawa. Martha imagined clear, running water rushing through deep subterranean ravines. It seemed to her that as one part of the city was uncovered, cleaned up and put on show, shadows, ghosts and other precious things moved deeper beneath the surface. She knew Klara treasured the broken thing, the half-ruined or wrecked. Klara knew the disintegrating buildings and places that kept the shadows and ghosts safe. She had told Martha that there was so much to show her, places that were out of the way or that people had forgotten about or did not know, places way beyond the reach of the newly improved roads. She wanted to take Martha to the forest and the marshes in the east, to see the remains of what had once been and was now abandoned. Martha said yes to everything. She would go anywhere. She would follow Klara into the most remote wilderness. She would go on any adventure, she would travel on trains across the steppe, stuck in sleeping cabins with drunks. She would go on foot or by bus or by car.

Late the following morning, they drove to the market to buy berries and vegetables. As they sailed through an intersection, Klara pointed out a street corner that had once been the boundary of the Ghetto. Martha turned quickly but only saw a large green billboard advertising a supermarket on the wall of an old building. She knew that before the war, this part of the city had been the garment district. She had read about narrow streets lined with factories, warehouses and crowded tenements. In small workshops and in back rooms, fabric was cut, sewn, fitted and pressed. This poorest and oldest part of the city was sealed off soon after the city was occupied and remained so until the end of the war. The non-Jewish poor were deported or forced to live elsewhere and Jews from other areas of the city and its surroundings were forced into the Ghetto. Martha knew from her father, who was eleven when the war began, that the school he attended had been shut down and turned into police headquarters and that his family left their large apartment after their neighbours warned them that they would soon be evicted. They packed their belongings and left, never quite sure whether the neighbours wanted to take over their apartment or whether they had managed to evade being thrown out in the middle of the night with only a few minutes to grab what they could. Martha's father, uncle and grandfather moved into a shed on a plot of land just outside the city. The rest of the family moved into a small, nearby flat. Martha's father gathered old textbooks from his sisters and brother and went for lessons at the apartment of an old, half-paralysed professor who had agreed to teach a few students in secret. When Martha's father turned fourteen and had to earn a ration card, his uncle found him a job as a junior assistant in an architectural office. Every day on his way to work, he passed a section of the Ghetto. He saw a city within a city enclosed with barbed wire fences, guarded day and night, secret yet visible. He saw people taken there surrounded by police or guards. Empty trucks drove in through guarded gates and left, laden with soldiers' uniforms and other goods made by the people living inside. Towards the end of the war, large groups of Jews were taken out and transported to no one knew where. No one ever heard of them being relocated anywhere, no one saw them again.

In his job as a junior assistant in the architectural office, Martha's father took measurements of the existing buildings along the main pedestrian thoroughfare and occasionally made a sketch from the measurements. The tenements had two long wings with a very long and narrow courtyard between them; courtyards as narrow as intestines, he would say. The entire city was to be remodeled, beginning with the modernisation of the five-kilometre central thoroughfare. The plans of the existing buildings were taken to the new chief architect. The new chief architect drew up plans for large, spacious apartments to be built for the new German population. The two adjoining wings of every existing tenement building were to be demolished to make a green space, and the two wings of the next building would be joined by covering the courtyard to make large apartments. Martha's father always smiled when he said that the plans for the remodelled city were never realised. At the end of the war, the buildings on the central thoroughfare remained the same as they had been when his two older sisters used to stroll along the pavement arm in arm before the war.

Klara parked the car some distance from the market. She left the engine running until the sad, strange love song playing on the radio had finished. It was sung by one of Klara's favourite singers. He had visited Czawa, the country of his forebears, several times and performed many concerts. As they walked towards the market, Klara said that one summer, the singer had spent weeks in his room writing the song for his lover. His lover spent the weeks watching films and reading and waiting for him to come out of his room. Whenever she knocked on the door, the song was not yet ready, needed more work, was not quite right. Finally, the song was finished and the singer came out of his room ready to play his guitar, calling out to his beloved. He waited but there was no reply. Klara laughed. His beloved had packed her bags and left. Klara suddenly stopped then beckoned. They turned sharply into a gateway off the street. Martha followed her into a courtyard bordered on three sides by tenement buildings. The inside wall of the gateway was covered in soccer graffiti; racist, anti-Semitic, it made no sense to Martha. There was a smell of old piss. The courtyard was deserted. She looked down at the cracked uneven paving that hinted at a pattern, at an underlying connection between the many worn paving stones and cobble stones she had seen in Nadwodom, in Nice, in Melbourne. They stood still for a moment then went further into the courtyard. Klara whispered that you could hide in these old buildings. Over the years, people had built partitions, false walls and attics within attics; an entire network of hiding spots. You could hide in the basement, in the cellar, in dark corners and in corridors where you could flatten yourself against the wall and disappear.

When they got to the market, they moved briskly from stall to stall, Martha always two steps behind Klara. They bought what they needed and wandered back to the car. Klara turned the ignition key and the car engine gasped, grated, turned over, then stopped. She turned the key twelve times before the car finally jerked forward and took off. Klara drove fast along the narrow and uneven roads, as if the momentum would keep them going.

As they approached a sharp bend in the road, she pointed at a narrow, decrepit-looking building directly ahead. Martha pressed herself against the back of the car seat and thrust both feet forward as they sped towards the building. Klara said she thought that was the tenement where Martha's father used to live. She had read somewhere that it was scheduled to be demolished but she didn't know when. She turned the steering wheel sharply to the right and they whizzed past. Martha looked back at the rundown building where her father may or may not have lived. She was surprised that Klara wasn't sure whether it was the right building or not. There didn't seem to be any way of making sure. The current inhabitants would have no idea who had lived there all those years ago and now it seemed the building would soon be gone. Klara said she would bring Martha back in the next few days to take photographs. They would take photographs from inside the courtyard and then go into the building and take photographs from the first-floor landing window. They could even knock on the door of the first floor apartment. Martha nodded as they raced past restored tenement buildings painted in bright colours with small, curved, ornate balconies, decorative window casements and round attic windows.

The decorated facades reminded Martha of the illustrations in her favourite children's book of poems. The book was a present from her grandparents and had arrived in a large brown parcel. There was a picture of a buxom blonde woman with a necklace of round multi-coloured beads leaning out of a small ornate window, her mouth shaped in a perfect "O" singing tra la la. Martha's father remembered some of the poems from his early childhood. He recited a poem about a man searching for the glasses perched on his nose. Then he told the only story Martha ever heard him tell about his childhood before the war. It was about a school excursion to one of the biggest textile factories in

Nadwodom. The children were led through several large halls. Each hall was dedicated to one kind of machine, each type of machine had its own environment. One hall was full of steam and in another, the steady clacking of the machinery drowned out every other sound. In every space there was constant movement. People moved around the machines, keeping time with them, tending to them. Martha's father was overwhelmed by this powerful place. About mid-morning, as the school children made their way back to the entrance in a line of two abreast, they were asked to stop and wait. The heavy, ornate wrought iron gates of the factory opened and the engineer's carriage rolled in. The children watched the engineer descend from the carriage. An assistant rushed towards him. They conferred for a moment, then the assistant escorted the engineer to the front office. The teacher explained that the engineer was responsible for all the machines and that after he inspected the factory and surveyed the workings of the machinery, he would return to his office to make calculations for improvements. The moment Martha's father saw the carriage sweep through the factory gates he decided to become an engineer. When her father finished telling the story, Martha went back to her room with the book of poetry for children. As she sat turning the pages, examining the illustrations, letting the deep colours seep into her, she decided to become an artist.

Klara quickly turned her head, glanced at Martha then looked back at the road.

"If your parents had not left, if they had stayed here, then you would have been born in Nadwodom and we would have known each other all our lives," she said.

Martha nodded at Klara's profile.

"If I had been born in Nadwodom and grown up here, this

would be my city and we would be like sisters."

"We are sisters."

They now travelled along a main road. They turned the corner at the light into a busy highway and a moment later the car stopped. Klara tried to start the engine several times, but nothing happened. "We'll have to push the car. I'll steer and you push from behind," she said. Martha looked at the traffic streaming past. She got out slowly and sidled around to the back of the car. Klara was half in and half out of the car with one hand steering. They both pushed and the car slowly rolled forward but instead of steering the car towards the curb, Klara put on the left-hand indicator and steered the car into the centre of the highway. Martha stopped pushing and looked behind. A bus and cars sped towards them. She froze, certain they would be run down. Klara called out that her mechanic lived just around the corner. "Are you afraid?" she asked. Martha nodded. Klara dived into the car, reached into the glove compartment, pulled out a fluorescent safety jacket and threw it over to Martha. The bus roared past them. Martha closed her eyes and pushed. A cyclist stopped and the three of them pushed the car into the side street.

The following morning, the mechanic rang and said the car had stopped because it ran out of petrol. Klara said she could never tell how much petrol she had because the petrol gauge had got stuck and would jump all over the place. She picked up the car late in the morning and as soon as she returned, insisted that they drive to the building where she thought Martha's father used to live. They drove without talking and parked the car a street away from the rundown tenement. As they walked towards the dirty facade with sections of peeling paint that reminded Martha of camouflage, Klara said she was almost certain it was the right building. Martha kept her camera in her bag until they stood right before the building then she took it out and held it loosely, like a stone she had picked up on a walk. She felt that she ought to take a number of photographs, but now she wasn't sure why and she wasn't sure that the photographs would mean anything anyway. She sensed Klara watching her. She held up the camera. She would take a couple of photographs of the building to show her father. First, she took a photo of the doorway. Then she tried to frame a section of wall with peeling yellow paint, the paving stones in the courtyard and a window. It was not possible. She focused on each element one by one and pressed the button on the camera. Then she stepped back and looked up. A pot of red geraniums stood on the ledge of a first-floor window. The window was half-open and there was no curtain, but she couldn't see inside. She had once asked her father who had lived in the apartment before his family moved in, but he had no idea. A government office allocated empty apartments to those who had nowhere to live and there had been many empty apartments when the Occupation ended. Martha put the camera back in her bag. Klara said they could always come back later. She said they could spend a day taking photographs of her favourite old buildings and one of the few remaining factory sites, and then return at night to photograph the old doorways and courtyards again. Martha stood close to Klara, their shoulders touching, and said that was just what she had wanted to do all along.

They returned to the car and drove to a recently restored mansion that had just been reopened to the public. The Neo-Renaissance villa was built in 1875 by Frederik Werner, one of the most powerful and affluent textile industrialists of the late nineteenth century. Werner had built a four storey brick factory, a spinning mill, a weaving mill and a housing district for the workers who had swarmed into the city from the surrounding countryside. As the textile factory expanded, so did the workers' district. It included shops, an elementary school, hospital, pharmacy and a fire station. Some people spent their entire lives in the district and never ventured into the town. The factory workers' housing radiated out from the extensive gardens that surrounded the industrialist's villa. The huge factory also stood nearby; close enough for Frederik Werner to hear the morning siren while he sat at the breakfast table.

As they approached the mansion, Klara pointed out the workers' tenements that had been neglected for decades but had recently undergone renovations and were now sought-after places to live. The white windowsills and doors gleamed beside the clean dark brick walls. As they stood at an intersection waiting to cross the road, Martha noticed a black and white cat standing on the shiny white ledge of a second storey window. On either side of the cat were pots of red, white and pink geraniums. The window was partially open, but the room inside was screened by a white lace curtain. Martha lagged behind Klara, considering whether to take a photograph of the cat on the window ledge amongst the flowers. It would have been a postcard kind of picture, giving an impression of calmness and of being somehow out of time. Klara called out that they needed to hurry if they were to see both the villa and the exhibition of modern art in the renovated stables.

The interior of the museum was dark, opulent and oppressive. The floorboards creaked as Martha and Klara walked from room to room. A portrait of the industrialist hung on a burgundy wall beside the portrait of his wife. Below the portrait, a bronze bust of his oldest son stood on a carved wooden pedestal. Everything looked heavy. Martha scanned the pamphlet handed to them when they bought entrance tickets. It included an anecdote about the industrialist's youngest daughter. She was so dear to her father that whenever she felt unwell, Werner arranged for hay to be strewn on the streets surrounding the villa gardens so that the noise of horses and carts would not disturb her. Martha stood in the doorway of the daughter's room and gazed at the objects inside. Near the entrance was a painting of a young girl. Next to the stove heater, there was a high metal bed and a bathing corner with a washbowl sitting on a marble top. Above it hung an ornate oval mirror and nearby were a small table, chairs, a couch and armchairs. It was like looking into an oversized doll's house, into the crowded bedroom of a doll child.

When Klara and Martha had had enough of the oppressive interior, they went out into the garden. Instead of visiting the art museum in the redesigned stables, they walked back to the street. They waited for the light to change at the same intersection they had crossed on their way in and Martha looked up at the second floor window of the renovated tenement. The black and white cat was now lying on the inside window ledge behind the pots of flowers. She told Klara to go on ahead and then took out her camera. She ran across the road and stood directly opposite the window. In quick succession, she turned on the camera, held it up and pressed the silver button. She shoved the camera back in her bag and ran after Klara.

That evening Martha was so tired that as soon as they got home, she went to her bedroom, dropped her bag on the bed and flopped down beside it. She lay flat on her back for a few minutes then reached for her bag and took out the camera. She had taken several photos inside and outside the mansion museum and she wanted to see the photograph of the cat. She turned on the camera and the first photograph she saw on the screen was a picture she had not taken. She expected to see a black and white cat lying just inside a white window ledge with pots of geraniums on either side. Instead, she saw a girl standing at the window between the lace curtains. The girl was looking down at the street or at something just before her or perhaps just thinking. She was about eleven years old with long sandy hair parted on the side and a serious, proprietorial expression. Her mouth was slightly downturned, as if she was a little sulky or cross. There was no cat. Martha stared at this girl who could have been from the nineteenth century or the twentieth century. She could have been some kind of manifestation of the industrialist's daughter transported into a factory worker's flat or the ghost of a factory worker's daughter who would soon be a textile factory worker herself. Martha looked away from the girl. The geraniums, the windowsill, the brickwork all seemed solid. She glanced at the image of the girl again, half expecting her to look up, wanting her to move, to stand aside even so that she could see inside the room. She peered more closely at the slightly surly face then turned off the camera. She considered what might have happened. A girl had come to take the cat away from the window at the exact moment that Martha had pressed the button to take the photograph or the girl had come to the window and the cat had moved away as Martha pressed the button. Either way, something had disappeared, and something had appeared in its place or had taken its place. A transformation had occurred to produce a photograph that was a number of photographs. The more she thought about it, the more it seemed that she could be looking at an eleven-year-old Klara or a version of Klara transposed into another time. She even saw herself at the age of eleven. She turned off the camera and put it in her suitcase.

In the late morning of the following day, Martha sat by the window in Klara's little upstairs kitchen and looked down on the square of bright green garden. Beyond the two sheds at the back of the garden was a path through the small forest reserve to the tram that went to Central Nadwodom. Ever since she arrived, Martha had found it hard to get her bearings. She followed Klara, noted everything and still had no sense of the shape of the city. Even if they marked out the most intricate and detailed map, she doubted that she would be able to grasp it. In four weeks, there was not enough time to see anything properly, to see anything through, to see through anything. She would have to come back again and again, she would have to come back hundreds of times to get her bearings. She checked the time. Klara had gone to the University to get copies of some documents and they had arranged to meet in the afternoon at the Museum of Modern Art. Martha finished her cup of tea, picked up her bag and jacket and walked down the side of the house to the path that led through the forest reserve to the tram stop. She had never gone anywhere on her own in Nadwodom apart from buying bread and cheese from the local shop. She knew exactly where the path would take her but felt uneasy, as if there was a path that looked exactly the same but would take her to somewhere completely unknown.

When Martha was four, her mother went to the hospital for a procedure to do with veins and her grandmother travelled by tram from the other side of the city to stay with them. In the morning, Martha and her grandmother left the house in the direction of the kindergarten. Martha knew they had to turn into one street, then another and that eventually they would come to a kind of forest. They walked down the hill, crossed the main road but then turned left into a street that was unfamiliar to Martha. They walked up the hill into unknown territory. Martha's grandmother held Martha's hand and was silent. Eventually they heard children's voices up ahead. They crossed a road and came to a school. They peered at the playground through the wire mesh fence. Children ran around throwing balls, chasing one another and then Martha spotted Angela. Martha waved and Angela ran to the fence and jumped. The tips of her shoes poked through the wire mesh and she hoisted herself up. Martha's grandmother opened her bag and gave Martha a lolly to give to Angela. Then they turned and went back down the hill. They walked and walked until they were back at the busy road. They tried again and went in the opposite direction. This time, Martha was more certain and led the way. They continued to the forest and when they found a bench, they sat and rested. From where they sat, they could see the forests on the other side of the frontier. If they walked through those forests, the first person they came across would greet them in a foreign language. Martha chewed the lolly her grandmother gave her then they got up and walked along the path away from the forest. They turned a corner and Martha recognised the gate of the kindergarten. Her grandmother opened her handbag and gave Martha a clean white handkerchief. Martha ran through the gate and through the open door of the classroom. Children moved around packing up; kindergarten had finished. Martha crept out and ran back towards the street. She stood at the gate and watched her grandmother's very straight back recede down the tree-lined street.

The tram travelled a short distance through the forest reserve then down a boulevard towards the main pedestrian promenade and passed a series of Secession style buildings. An almost ridiculously small tower protruded from the grey slate tiled roof of one of the buildings the tram seemed to crawl past. In the centre of the tower was a small, white-edged oval window decorated with masonry garlands, as if made for someone to lean out of and begin singing. The tram travelled through an area Martha didn't recognize. Without thinking, she jumped up and pressed the button by the back door to get off before there was no way back. She stood on the street and realized she had got off way too soon. Now she had to decide which way to go. When she finally got to the art museum, she found that it was closed on that day, although the cafe and the adjoining bookshop were open. She sat in a lounge chair by a window in the café and since she didn't know how long Klara would be, prepared to wait a while. She gazed out the window and wondered what it would be like if Klara came to Australia. She found it hard to imagine. They would both become different people. Klara would become transparent, voiceless, like a ghost unable to step firmly on the ground, unable to leave a footprint. They would have to travel all the time. They would sit side by side on a plane, in a train, on a bus and as they spoke their private language, they would both become invisible, shielded by the sounds that no one around them understood. They would travel like this from place to place, staying as long or as short a time as they wished until they returned to Czawa.

Klara arrived at the café half an hour later. She was surprised that the art museum wasn't open but pleased they could sit in the cafe. She bought two small vodkas to celebrate; she had applied for a job with a research unit working in the north eastern marshes and she was told she would get it. They raised their glasses and drank the honey flavoured vodka for good luck. They ordered coffee and cake and just as Martha was beginning to sink into the lounge chair, Klara asked about her writing project. She wanted to know about the Australian photographer Martha hinted at from time to time. Martha looked down and then glanced sideways at the window. She hesitated then drew herself up to try and conjure Marion Porter. She began with the eight cardboard boxes, marked 'From the estate of Marion Porter' that had been delivered to the Library and left around a table near her desk. Martha had opened the first box and saw it contained a number of exhibition invitations and exhibition catalogues, a few letters, two exercise books full of notes, three sketches and a pile of photographs. Everything had been mixed up, as if someone had cleared a room in a hurry and threw whatever they came across into the box. The Manuscripts Librarian asked Martha to sort through all eight boxes and make a preliminary list. Martha learned that Marion Porter, born 1905 died 1992, had been a photographer who lived in Melbourne for most of her life. Although she was never famous, she was highly regarded in certain artistic circles and her photographs were sought after. As she sorted the stuff in the boxes, she wondered whether Marion kept these bits and pieces for so many years because they meant something to her or because she just didn't get around to sorting through everything she had accumulated or because she didn't like to throw anything out and no longer knew what was there. Somehow the papers she had kept and the notes she had written, the sketches and the family photographs became important because they had not been thrown out. They took on a life of their own – Marion Porter's friends and acquaintances. Martha spent more time than she should have looking through the diaries which had such irregular, documentary style entries and yet were so intimate and intense. By skimming through the diaries and letters, she worked out that Marion Porter had lived most of her life alone. When her mother had a stroke late in life, Marion moved in with her and looked after her until she died. Before that, she had lived in a house that her parents had bought as a holiday house but never stayed in. It was close to the beach in the suburb of Black Rock and had once been an old fisherman's cottage, a boarding house and then a shop. It was this dwelling that interested Martha. Marion took hundreds of photographs of the building. She took photographs of the doorways and the staircase and the windows as if the place might disappear or as if she was documenting traces of what it had been in the past, as if she was trying to capture clues as delicate as the movement of a lace curtain. Sometimes Marion arranged her photographs against a dark purple backing cloth and displayed them in the front window for passersby to see, not for people to buy or ask about them, just to see them as they passed. When Porter was very old, she used to go down to a nearby parking lot and photograph the backs of buildings that were being demolished. She hardly ever took photographs of human subjects. She liked to capture the traces people left behind, to point to the spaces where their shadows remained. It seemed to Martha that Marion could capture fragility. She could bring out the already present deterioration in the places where people lived and worked and came together.

Martha told Klara that when she read or wrote about Marion Porter, she often thought about photographing Nadwodom. Klara said four weeks was too short for such a project, especially if half the time was spent visiting other relatives and friends. She had once worked for a researcher taking photographs of a few buildings destined for demolition or renovation and it had taken months. Martha would have to come back and stay for at least three months. Klara picked up her coffee cup and said they could make plans and do preliminary work since she had already done something similar. Martha murmured that yes, she would come back for several months and they could make something together. "We could produce a book of images and photographs of Nadwodom... or we could have an exhibition," her voice became distant and trailed off. She thought of Marion Porter standing in a courtyard, looking into a box camera; she was the perfect guide to shadow.

Just before they reached the tram stop on their way home,

Klara told Martha to look back. Martha looked over her shoulder at a parking lot. She could just make out some kind of stone monument. "That's where the Great Synagogue used to be," Klara said. "It was one of the richest and largest synagogues." They stood and stared at the empty space of the parking lot. "It was burned to the ground by the Nazis. Everything inside, Torah Scrolls, silver ornaments, works of art, everything was burned. Now there is nothing there." Martha waited for Klara to say more, as if there had to be more, as if that couldn't be it, but Klara walked on in the direction of the tram stop. Martha followed, wanting to learn more of what had disappeared, what had been lost. She thought they ought to stand still for a little longer to see if they could sense something, but they had already moved on.

That night Martha and Klara went to a poetry performance in a nightclub. The place was crowded by the time they arrived, but they managed to sit at a table wedged in by a window with thick orange-tinted glass. On stage were two old, dark brown harmoniums and two large palms. The palms hinted at the tropics while the tinted glass made it possible to imagine deep winter. They leaned towards one another across the table. In winter, they would go out at night dressed in heavy coats and fur-lined Cossack boots and walk along streets packed with snow and ice. The snow would creak under their feet and the sharp air would sting their nostrils with every breath.

A man walked onto the stage and set one harmonium in motion, then the other. The harmoniums heaved in the same tempo, slowly and rhythmically, like a pair of lungs producing a low continuous note, a thread of breath that underpinned everything that followed. A musician carrying a clarinet appeared on stage followed by a woman. The woman knelt on a cushion between the instruments. Now there was a deep rumbling from the harmoniums and a high-pitched melody from the clarinet. The woman sang the first poem in a language Martha did not understand. Each poem she sang was in a different language and style from the one preceding it. Towards the end of the performance, she began a poem in a whisper, as if all the other poems had been leading up to this one. The whispered words became imperceptibly louder and stronger until the singer's voice filled the entire room with one long note that sounded like a cry and ebbed away as imperceptibly as it had started. Martha and Klara looked at each other and shivered at this lament for the city, this echo of persecution and despair. They left the nightclub and walked back to the car side by side, moving in tandem as if they were one person split.

The next day, Klara wanted to go on a trip out of the city. Before Martha got up, she had arranged for her friend, Ola, to come and pick them up. They decided to visit the oldest remaining Romanesque church in Czawa. Ola thumped up the stairs half an hour late because her baby hadn't wanted to let her go. They waited for Martha to finish her coffee and then she followed them downstairs. She sat in the front seat of Ola's new, imported car. Ola spoke good English because she had lived in Switzerland for two years. She had worked as a housekeeper for a famous scientist. A friend of a friend could no longer do the job and wanted someone to take her place, so Ola went and that's where she met Eric, the son of a world-renowned chemist and the father of her baby son. It was good money and the old scientist was pleasant enough. His son Eric often came to stay and although he was in his late fifties, he looked like a man of thirty. He had been a drug addict from his youth and never worked, but he was charming and they fell in love. When she returned to Czawa, he went with her but because of his rehabilitation programme he had to go back to Switzerland every six weeks.

The old scientist had a stroke that left him partially paralysed and unable to speak soon after Ola left the household. She still spoke to him most days either by phone or on Skype with her son on her knee. He remained silent while she talked, but she knew the calls kept him alive.

About half an hour after they left the outskirts of the city, Klara pointed at a stork's nest on the roof of a cottage. Ola stopped the car and Martha and Klara jumped out to have a closer look. As they approached the cottage, Klara stopped suddenly and put her arm out in front of Martha. Two storks stood side by side on a straw bale. The birds stood so still they could have been museum exhibits. The birds observed the humans and the humans observed the birds and no one moved until Martha and Klara backed away towards the car. Klara explained how storks liked to nest and breed in open grassland. In the Middle Ages, woodland was cleared, and new pastures and farmland were created, making a good habitat for the birds. Since industrialisation and changes in farming, however, there were less and less of them. Still, every August and September, storks flew south to Africa where they spent the winter in savannah and in spring they returned north. All the storks set off southward in an inherited direction and only looked for a new wintering location if the weather was bad. In spring, all the storks, no matter where they'd been, found their way back to their traditional breeding sites.

Ola stopped the car near the Romanesque church and Klara went to the entrance to see if there was a guide around. Martha stayed in the car while Ola drove into the carpark. As she drove, Ola said that she supposed Martha knew that Klara hardly made any money from her archaeological work and that she had no work at the moment. Martha nodded. Ola said she gave Klara money from time to time for petrol and to pay bills. She could only do that because Eric gave her money when he went to Czawa every month, but she couldn't always manage it. Martha nodded. It struck her that she had no sense of Klara's day to day existence, that of course her visit was an aberration, a special event. She felt ashamed that she had forgotten to give Klara money for petrol and bills. Klara emerged from the entrance of the church with a middle-aged woman beside her. She waved at Martha to come over. The woman was a volunteer guide, an art historian who spoke a little English. Klara had arranged for the woman to give them a tour together with another small group from Canada. The guide said she could give the highlights in English, but Martha said she didn't need to and offered to translate for the four Canadians. They followed the guide into the church. She pointed out the portal framed by adoring angels and asked them to sit in the pew. In a soft voice, she reminded them that they were in a church then explained that the building was built in the form of a basilica with an aisle and galleries. She pointed out the twin-tower west facade and two apses. She explained the characteristics of a collegiate church. Every now and then, Martha turned to the four Canadian tourists and quietly summarised in English what the guide had said. After a while, Martha tried to keep the same rhythm and pace as the guide. Sometimes she struggled to catch the right word or to find the right phrase, but she kept going and then, all of a sudden, without realising it, she took off in the wake of the guide's words. She stood, swivelled and flung one arm towards the east and the other towards the west, comparing the features of the western end of the church to the eastern end. She flew, propelled by the current of words that passed through her like an electric charge. She soared, as light as a sheet of paper, maintaining a perfect balance between one language and the other. She had become a fine and sensitive membrane, responding to the vibrations of words, transforming them as they passed through her. She and the guide spoke in tandem, as though she would at any moment, overtake the guide and speak in both languages, one laid over the other. The guide asked her to please sit down and remember where she was, then insisted Martha sit down and lower her voice. Martha dropped onto the wooden bench with a clunk. Klara giggled and winked. Martha sat silent for a moment, but like a child skipping and chanting the words that keep her moving, she couldn't stop. She continued the translation in a loud whisper, punctuating the guide's longer sentences with her own.

The north portal was the oldest part of the church and dated back to the first half of the twelfth century. Martha demurely drew the Canadians' attention to the sculptures and to the big arch as the guide pointed them out. Then they all stood in single file and went, one by one, to the base of the big arch and stood with an ear pressed to the cold stone. The guide stood at the other end of the arch with her back to them and whispered into the stone. The person standing with their ear pressed against the opposite arch could hear her words as clearly as if she were standing before them or the stone were speaking. This was how lepers had confessed their sins to the priests. When it was her turn, Martha closed her eyes and listened, waiting for the ancient voice trapped inside the stone to speak.

When everyone had their turn standing at the base of the arch listening to the guide whisper, the guide walked to the centre of the portal and gathered them together. With an embarrassed smile, she told them a folk tale about the local devil. According to one story, it was taking a very long time to build the church because the granite stones needed for building were so heavy. While the local people were still gathering the stones, a devil fell in love with a peasant girl and followed her everywhere. In order to help build the church, she asked the devil if he would carry the heavy stones to build an inn where they could drink and dance. The devil agreed and moved all the stones in one day but when he realised that he had carried stones to build a church and not an inn, he vowed to destroy the building. He tried to overturn one of the church towers but could not, so he turned to the other tower and tried so hard that the fingerprints from his great paws and the outline of one of his horns and tail can still be seen on the external west wall.

They circled the church, then left it and the group of Canadians behind. Klara and Ola led Martha to the nearby archaeological dig. Klara swayed slightly in her wedge-heeled sandals as they walked along a narrow path bordered on either side by thick, bright green grass as high as their waists. They passed a sign that forbade entry to the site and stopped before a shallow square marked out with stakes and string. Klara waved to a couple of workers digging in the square, then went to look for the supervisor of the dig. Martha and Ola stayed back and watched the workers crouching in the neat square pits, digging with trowels or using various sorts of measuring and recording instruments. It looked as if they were working on a small building site but instead of building, the workers were carefully dislodging and examining whatever small pieces they found. They picked out the smallest fragments they could uncover, further taking apart what had already disintegrated.

Klara came back with a short dark-haired man with a thick drooping moustache that made him look like a nobleman from the nineteenth century. He spoke to Klara and Ola and joked in an easy way without looking at Martha. When Klara introduced Martha as her cousin from Australia, he vaguely acknowledged her and continued to explain that once they had finished their excavation work, there would be a project to reconstruct the parts of the settlement that were from the sixth century. When Martha asked how the settlement had come to disappear, he looked at her as if she were a child too young to understand.

That night, Martha thought of writing a letter to Tom. Although they had been living in different cities for years, they wrote to each other every now and again or met up if they were in the same city. She had sent Tom a brief email to say she was going to Czawa and he had asked her to write. She hadn't so far. She flipped to a blank page of the green notebook she had bought a couple of weeks before she left Melbourne. Instead of writing a letter, she wrote about the devil who destroyed the sixth century settlement. 'The local devil, who was believed to be the lord of the castle, disliked the idea of having the huge church so close to him, so he tried to get rid of it several times. Eventually, he decided to turn the church into an inn. To do that, he needed some big stones that he had to bring from a distance. At midnight one night, on his way back flying high in the clouds and carrying heavy stones, he heard a cock crow. He dropped the stones and they fell on the buildings of the nearby wooden settlement, crushing them. Now the huge stones lie scattered in the fields as if they had always been there.'

~

Towards the end of her stay, Martha visited her mother's youngest sister, Eva, who lived in a city on the other side of Czawa. When she returned to Nadwodom, Uncle Andrew and Aunt Barbara, insisted she come over for dinner. She had only been away for a few days, but her uncle opened his arms and greeted her as if she had been away for years. "It's too early for you to go back, you need to stay for a full year to experience all the seasons." He stood in the doorway smiling, arms up and out like a tree. Martha laughed, unsure whether to step forwards or backward. She waited for him to move. Uncle Andrew stepped aside and swept his arm out to usher her in. Martha sat at the dining table and listened to Uncle Andrew describe his day. Nearly every day since he retired, he caught a tram into the town centre. On the way, he got off at every second stop to either visit someone or to wander around or to go into a shop or café. After several hours he would return home and describe what he had seen, who he had visited and what he had learned. Martha smiled and nodded and ate as quickly as she could, desperate to get back to Klara's place, to see her and to show her the sheet of grid paper with the hastily written names and notes their aunt Eva had given her.

When Martha finally went up the stairs to Klara's place, she found Klara and her friend Anton lounging on cushions on the big pull-out sofa. Anton had installed a new light fitting on the landing and they were talking about laying tiles in the bathroom. As Martha entered the room, Klara pointed out the white, beaded construction Anton had installed and that for some reason, made Martha think of a full moon. Martha hoped that Anton would leave soon so that she could show Klara the sheet of grid paper and tell her what she'd heard from their aunt. Klara pulled an armchair close to the sofa and gave Martha a small glass of vodka. She refilled Anton's glass. Martha sat deep in the armchair. It struck her that instead of spending her last few days in Nadwodom, exploring the city with Klara, looking for old, neglected buildings and gateways in preparation for their photography project, they could spend hours talking. Instead of taking their time looking down stairways into cellars, peering into courtyards, discovering compositions where they least expected it, they would rush to see an exhibition or a performance Klara had heard about and then be swept away in yet another direction. While Martha sat brooding, thinking she would have to plan their project in Melbourne, Anton asked what they had been doing since Martha arrived. Klara mimicked the prim voice of the guide in the Romanesque church, "Excuse me madam, excuse me, would you please sit down?" She said Martha took off and flew around the ancient church, waving her arms and talking like the wind. Anton asked what had made her so happy. Martha shrugged. All she knew was, suddenly, she'd been able to move effortlessly from one language to the other. She'd known what to say without thinking, completely taken over by the words. Anton wanted to know whether she dreamed in one language or the other or both? Martha sank deeper into the armchair. She didn't know what to say except that she had never thought about it. She half-closed her eyes, sank even further into the armchair and told them the dream she'd had a couple of weeks before she left Melbourne. "I was in a cinema. I was a child, a teenager and myself now. I was watching a black and white film made in the 1950s projected on a large cinema screen. It was the story of my mother's life played by my mother as a young woman. At one point, my mother had her head slightly turned away and looked down as if she was deep in thought. I saw her face from below and it seemed very large, as if I was in the front row of the cinema looking up at the huge screen. Then I realised I was also in the film. I was watching, working out what was happening in the film and playing my part all at the same time. My head became thick and heavy, clogged with words and sentences like wet sponges. I had to wake up so I could breathe."

Martha edged out of the armchair. She said she had to go to bed because she was very tired. She went to the bathroom and let water gush out of the tap while she cleaned her teeth. Then she went to the bedroom and crept up to the wall. She pressed her ear to the wall and listened to Klara's muffled voice. Klara was telling Anton about a dream she once had that still stayed with her. Martha held her breath and listened. Klara had found herself at the base of a steep, narrow and decrepit wooden staircase. She had to climb the crumbling stairs to get to a safe place to spend the night. With great effort, she went up each step and felt the step beneath fall away. Sometimes a step disintegrated as she put her foot on it so that she had to cling to the tower wall. She finally reached the empty and bare place where she would sleep. There were other people occupying similar spaces. They kept to themselves, no one seemed to know each other, and no one spoke. As soon as she found a place to sit on the floor, she realised that she wouldn't be able to go down the way she came up. There was no rest and no safe place. Martha recognised the recurring dream she too used to have years ago, but couldn't remember ever telling Klara about it. In the dream she dreaded but dreamt often, the walls of the tower were a sandy yellow and the wooden, sometimes stone, stairs were also a yellow ochre. Sometimes she didn't make it to the top. She found an alcove, like an outpost, where she could rest temporarily. At other times, she had to find her way down the disintegrating stairs and then begin the climb again almost immediately. Anton muttered something and Klara replied in a voice so low that Martha could not make out the words. She crept away from the wall.

A few weeks ago, she and Klara had stopped before an old gateway and looked at the pock marked surface covered in peeling paint. The muted ochres and pale blues seemed to have seeped out from the stone beneath and bled into one another, turning the old gateway into an abstract work of art, the richest work of art Martha had ever seen. She could have gazed at it for hours, at the layers of colour and peeling paint and pockmarked stone because they allowed glimpses of secrets, glimpses of life absorbed by the stone, absorbed by the building.

Martha took out her green notebook and got into bed. She had put the folded sheet of grid paper her aunt Eva had given her inside the front cover. She turned the first few pages of the notebook, which were covered in messy notes she had written before she'd left Melbourne. They included a description of where her father had once lived and his memory of measuring the old tenements that were to be remodeled during the war. She had recorded his memory of travelling on the tram that went through the Ghetto, of sitting in the back carriage where the non-Jewish citizens of Czawa were allowed to sit, of guards locking the doors. It was forbidden to approach the windows or to throw anything out, but he managed to see, to catch a glimpse of thin, ragged children pulling a cart. He saw trucks laden with materials driving into the Ghetto and he saw trucks piled high with boots and uniforms driving out. He heard that some people managed to shove a parcel of food through or under the high barbed fence that surrounded the entire old town. He heard of such things happening at night after the curfew. Martha wondered but did not ask if he might have seen Uncle Daniel and his sisters before they were deported to a concentration camp.

A week before she left Melbourne, on a grey and cold Sunday, Martha caught a tram to see an exhibition of photography at the Jewish Museum. The exhibition was called 'Dialogue' and aimed to explore Jewish history and tradition in Czawa and what Czawa meant to Holocaust survivors and their descendants. As the tram approached the museum, Martha became nervous. For many Jews living in Melbourne, their former homeland had become a place of death and horror once it had been occupied by Nazi Germany. She was afraid she would see Czawa as a tainted, ugly place. She shuffled into the museum. The woman behind the counter smiled. Martha hesitated as though she were waiting for a friend. She looked at her watch then smiled, shrugged and bought a ticket. The woman handed her a pamphlet, pointed down the corridor and said the exhibition continued upstairs. There were works by two photographers, one older, one younger, and a mixture of documentary and artistic photographs. The curator had written that the dark side of the story world known to the children of those who had emigrated, was persecution and the annihilation of their families, their friends and the places they had known.

Martha looked at the photographs taken by the older photographer. Most of his photographs were in colour and were taken in the mid-1980s. He had written that he had travelled to Czawa on a quest, driven to walk the streets of the old towns in Eastern Czawa, where his parents and forebears had once lived, as poets, singers, farmers and workers. There were often older people in the photographs, old peasant women or men in caps with creased, lively faces. There were no captions. Martha looked at the old wooden shutters hanging off rickety window frames. Sometimes a vase could be glimpsed behind a white lace curtain. She peered at a row of wooden houses with low pitched roofs, standing beside one another at the edge of a cracked pavement overgrown with bushes. The wood of the outer walls, worn over many decades, sometimes decorated with a carved lintel, made her think of the now invisible people who had once lived there. Many of the compositions included people in landscapes and played with light and shadow. It was as if the photographer knew the countryside, houses, streets and even people through stories and memories and longing, but at the same time found all this new and unfamiliar.

The more recent photographs were in black and white. There were many people in these photographs, both young and old, and most of the photographs had handwritten messages on them, as though scribbled in a hurry or with urgency. One or two messages were carefully composed, like poems. These photographs traced the recent 'revival' of Jewish life in Czawa since the late 1980s. Martha looked at the eager faces that seemed to invite others to join them; maybe you can come back, maybe you can even come and live here.

The woman who had sold Martha her ticket had been relieved from her duties at the counter and now wandered around the exhibition. There were not many people. Two small groups of three or so and a couple who were standing in the middle of the room talking to one another. The friendly guide approached Martha and asked if she had any connection to Czawa. Martha hesitated. She looked at the woman and blushed. Her hesitation was ridiculous. She blurted out that all her family had come from Czawa, that her uncle was Jewish, that... she made no sense. The woman smiled and looked at the photograph Martha had been looking at, a black and white photograph of a busy tram stop in Nadwodom in Autumn, then moved on. Martha stared at the photograph and wished she could have walked with the photographers, first one and then the other, and stood beside each of them while they decided what to photograph.

Klara knocked on the bedroom door and came in. Anton had gone. She asked Martha if she wanted a last drink. Martha shook her head. Klara sat on the edge of the bed.

"What did you want to show me? What did you bring back?"

Martha took out the sheet of grid paper and closed her notebook. She unfolded the paper and laid it out flat on the hard green cover. The paper was covered in hastily written names, some of which were circled and connected with lines, like an explorer's map showing a route through a series of islands. Aunt Eva had jotted down the names of the maternal side of their family, sometimes making a note, sometimes adding a question mark. Klara sat close beside her. Their aunt told Martha that neither she nor her older sisters were ever told anything about their family history. During their childhood, during the time of the Iron curtain, adults lowered their voices when they talked about the past for fear of something slipping out, of something being overheard, of something spreading or being misconstrued or used against the family, and then who knew what might happen to any of them. A child might tell another child who might tell a parent who was in the Party and who knew what connections people could have. When adults talked about what they had witnessed during the war or about the past and their families, they made sure the children were outside.

Aunt Eva said she'd put together stories from fragments she had gleaned over time. Since Martha seemed interested, she would tell her what she knew. Her great-grandmother's family had owned a large textile factory in a small town not far from Nadwodom. Klara shrugged. She had some vague notion that their great-grandmother had originated from a wealthy family. Martha pointed at their great-grandmother, Alina, on the sheet of paper, then moved across to Alina's brother, Theo. She wasn't sure if Theo was older or younger, but one Sunday when he was already an old man, he'd visited their grandparents. Aunt Eva was still a child and she made herself small in a corner by the door. She overheard Theo say that when he was little, every Saturday he and his sisters were told to be quiet around the house and to never go into their father's study. One Saturday, after they were told off for being too noisy, Theo and Alina dared each other to open the door to their father's study. Alina was their father's favourite. While they pretended to be playing hide and seek, she burst into the study, followed by Theo. They stopped and stared at their father sitting behind his desk with a shawl over his head and a large book opened before him. Years later, Theo realized the book must have been the Torah. Nothing was ever mentioned about this scene and the children never again approached the study on a Saturday. Klara had never heard the story, although she said it made sense. Klara knew that their great grandmother had fallen in love with the manager of her father's factory. Alina told her parents they wanted to get married, but both parents refused to allow it. Alina asked, demanded, insisted, begged, and when her parents still refused to give their permission, she arranged to meet up with her beloved Karl late at night and they eloped. Alina was immediately disinherited and cut off from the family. They moved to Nadwodom, into an apartment in a workers' tenement not far from Werner's textile factory. Karl worked as an assistant to a supervisor and during this time they had two sons. When their sons were both still in elementary school, Karl became sick with tuberculosis. In the last weeks that he was alive, when he could no longer leave his bed, he told his wife that when he died, she should go to his family in the village where he was born, one hundred kilometres from Nadwodom.

Karl died just as the First World War began. Alina arrived in his family village with her two young sons and Karl's parents took her in. They told her they did not have much to spare and that she would have to make do with what they could give her. As the war progressed, times became harder and there was less to eat. They sent her to an uncle's house. After a few months, the uncle let her know that she was a burden on the family, and they could no longer keep her and her sons. Alina gathered her boys and their few possessions, and they moved into a nearby cottage with an elderly widow. Although Alina had never made dresses for other people, she set herself up as a seamstress. She had a way with combining shapes and colours and soon had several customers. She found it hard to keep up with the dressmaking and after a couple of months, she set up a sewing class for the girls in the village and surrounding countryside. The young women flocked to the lady from the city to learn about style and fashion. One of her pupils was the daughter of a wealthy landowning peasant, a widower. He introduced himself to Alina and began to pay her visits. He was wealthy and lonely. He proposed to Alina and eventually she accepted. They went to the local priest to arrange the marriage. The priest refused to marry them because they came from such different worlds and were so far apart in education and manners that they would not be able to live together. The wealthy peasant was stubborn. They met with the priest four times and finally the priest relented. Just before the wedding, with money from her future husband, Alina sent her two sons to study in Nadwodom.

In the first three years of her marriage, Alina gave birth to two girls, the youngest was Martha and Klara's grandmother. Soon, just as the priest had predicted, Alina and her husband began to argue about everything and eventually they separated. At this time, her eldest son, barely into the second year of his studies in law, died from tuberculosis. The second son continued his studies in engineering but lived poorly and could not help his mother. When the girls were two and nearly four, Alina moved to the larger town of Malin not far from Nadwodom and set up another dressmaking school. This was where the family remained.

When Theo, who had also disowned his sister or at least had not helped her in any way, had to flee from the Eastern capital where he had moved with his family, Alina took him in. Just after the First World War, he led a successful battle against the attacking Soviet Army and became a hero. He was rewarded and given the post of Police Commander in the large easternmost district of the country. He owned an apartment block in the wealthiest part of the city and lived in the largest and best-appointed apartment. He was married and had three children. When his father died, his mother moved into an apartment next door. At the beginning of the Second World War, the Russians fought for the city and won it. Theo's apartment building was taken over. Late one afternoon, as he returned from the police headquarters, his caretaker came out just before he entered the gateway and warned him to keep away. She told him that his wife and their three children had already been captured and were on their way to the tundra plains in the far east. He would never see or hear of them again. The caretaker took him to a nearby house where her daughter was living, then helped him escape to Czawa. Theo, the caretaker and her daughter went to the town of Malin not far from Nadwodom.

Uncle Theo and the caretaker lived together, and her daughter became Uncle Theo's daughter. Aunt Eva said she had always noticed that while Uncle Theo sat at the table, his wife always sat on a stool close to the stove. When anyone got up to leave, she jumped up and stood by the door holding out their coats so that they could slip their arms into the sleeves. Klara shook her head; Theo's wife had been a caretaker all her life. She kept her place even when that place had disappeared long ago.

Aunt Eva had written a brief description of who people were beside some of the names on the sheet of grid paper. She noted that Martha's great-great-grandmother had died a year before her son, Theo, had to flee and that her gravestone was in the largest cemetery of that city, although no one in the family had ever seen it.

Klara said there was a line of strong-willed women on their mothers' side. She said that when Martha returned, they would have to work it all out, this half-known story that covered an entire era, that involved different communities and displaced people. Martha folded the square of grid paper and put it back into the notebook. Yes, they had it, a plan for another trip. The barely legible names, mapped out like an archipelago, promised any number of possibilities.

~

The next morning, Klara wheeled her bicycle out of the shed and Martha wheeled out a second bicycle that Anton had left behind. They rode along the uneven footpath then onto the wide, tree-lined road. Klara rode ahead, faster and faster. Martha followed, picking up speed, flying behind Klara like a kite. From time to time, Klara slowed down and looked over her shoulder. Martha shouted, hey, and peddled faster until she caught up and they rode abreast, calling out to one another like teenagers before Klara shot ahead again. They arrived at the Gallery of Modern Art, hot and flushed. Martha said that this time she wanted to actually look at the collection. "Of course, we must," said Klara and they went in. The Gallery seemed strangely empty. At the far end, a couple strolled towards the exit. Klara and Martha slowed down, taking their time surveying the room and what lay in it. Klara moved to a sculpture, Martha stood before printed works in a case and read the documentation on the wall. Bit by bit, they drifted apart until Martha found herself alone in the room. She stood before a metal and glass sculpture that seemed to have been placed out of the way by a window. Two asymmetrical halves of black metal were gently curved in different places, like swaying trees, and touched lightly but firmly at the top as if drawn together by some magnetic attraction. A curved glass pane arched over the metal like an inverted ski jump. Martha had the strange sensation of being on both sides of a window, looking at a window from behind swaying trees and at the same time standing at a window on the inside looking out. She peered at the card beneath the sculpture. The title was 'Construction', and the artist was Valeria Mrachko. Martha bent forward and peered beneath the curved glass pane into the spaces between the metal. A tiny, miniature person could creep inside and look out the window on the other side. Still hunched over, she circumnavigated the sculpture. Wherever she stood, the sculpture became completely different; a line became a point or a flat plane, what was curved became straight, what was wide became narrow. One moment there was a place to hide and the next the space was wide open.

"Hey."

Martha jumped. Klara appeared by her elbow. Side by side, they stood before the sculpture. Before Martha could ask about the artist, Klara told her what she knew. During the First World War, Mrachko had worked as a nurse in a Russian field hospital. She looked after a soldier from Czawa who had lost his leg. The soldier was also an artist. They fell in love, married and moved to Nadwodom, where Mrachko remained for the rest of her life. They were both very prolific and well-known artists. Mrachko gave birth to a daughter just as the Second World War began. They left Nadwodom for the Eastern provinces but returned within months. By then, their apartment had been confiscated and occupied. First, they found somewhere to live, then they searched for and saved a number of Mrachko's husband's paintings. They hid the paintings among the coal and potatoes in the cellar of the apartment building. Mrachko searched for her sculptures on her own. She found them in a dump in the outer suburbs. Bit by bit, she managed to secretly transport them back to the apartment building and hid them beside her husband's paintings. During the winter, they ran out of coal and wood. They had nothing to cook with and nothing to use for heating. The artist blamed his wife for not planning well enough to last the winter. He kept going on and on about how cold he was and how they couldn't even cook for their child. Finally, without saying a word, Mrachko went down to the cellar. She pulled out every one of her wooden sculptures and models and broke them up to use for firewood.

On their way out of the gallery, Martha left Klara in the foyer and went into the bookshop. She found a pamphlet about Mrachko and a couple of postcards. She paid for them quickly then shoved the pamphlet into her bag. She showed Klara the postcards but kept the pamphlet in her bag to add to the small, secret collection of objects she'd been keeping in the pocket of her suitcase, waiting for when she returned home.

In bed that night, she skimmed through the pamphlet and learned that Mrachko had worked as a drawing teacher once she and her husband separated after the war. Every morning, she and her young daughter walked through the park then across the forest reserve to the school. This forest reserve was the same one Martha and Klara walked through to get to the tram stop. One day, Mrachko went to a teachers' conference and was away longer than expected. Just before nightfall, her daughter walked to the forest to meet her. She walked along a path in the direction of the city and saw her mother in the distance. She smiled and waved then saw that her mother was staggering and holding on to her stomach as if she had been shot or stabbed. The daughter ran towards her mother and as she got closer, saw that her mother's shoes were soaked in blood and that blood was dripping down her legs. The daughter stood frozen, not knowing whether her mother had been attacked or had been in a terrible accident. She managed to get her mother home then called for help. Mrachko was rushed to the hospital and was diagnosed the next day with the cancer that would kill her in little over a year.

Martha fell asleep and dreamt that she stood before the Library where she worked. It was early evening, and the Library was lit up and busy, with people going in and out or hurrying past. Martha was going to the Library as a visitor, or as Adam Adler used to say, a reader. A workmate stood in the foyer. He was surprised to see her but said that as it happened an older couple had come in a little earlier asking to see her. He pointed up to the first floor and said they might still be there. She walked upstairs then looked down the aisles of bookshelves. In a narrow, badly lit aisle towards the back of the room, she saw her mother and father. They were looking at the spines of the books on the lower shelves, searching for something. They both seemed strangely diminutive, as if they had shrunk a little in order to fit in among the shelves. Before Martha could say anything, her mother turned and smiled at her, pleased that she had come to look for them and relieved that she had found them.

~

Three days before she left Nadwodom, Martha had a day to herself. The house was empty from early in the morning. Klara had gone out with her parents, something to do with sorting out their pension and taking them to their allotment out of town. Martha stood at the bedroom window with her face so close to the pane that her breath, trapped, returned and she could smell the stale, spent odour. It was an overcast day, a premonition of autumn. She looked down on the small square of lush, overgrown grass. The trees in the reserve towered over the row of white wooden sheds at the back of the garden as if pressing against them, pushing at the border between the garden and the forest. Martha considered whether to get a bike out of the shed and go for a ride or wander through the small section of forest behind the house and then go to the park or take a tram to the city. She put on one of Klara's light jackets, left the house and followed the path that led to the tram stop. The cool damp air that came off the trees soothed her face and she turned off the path to walk among them. Here the slice of forest on the urban fringe hinted at the presence of an ancient wilderness. In autumn, mushrooms usually appeared on the branches that had fallen to the ground or beneath mouldy leaves. Klara would know where to find them, what they were called, how to cook them. Even in the opposite hemisphere, where the plantation pine trees grew in straight lines like soldiers, the meaty orange-ringed mushrooms were hidden beneath mounds of brown pine needles. They needed the dark. They needed damp and dirt teeming with bacteria and when they were either pickled or fried in butter, they held the taste of the hidden parts of the forest. For Martha, the taste of mushrooms held the experience of crouching, sweeping aside pine needles and cutting firm fleshy mushroom stems with a small sharp knife. Beside the large mushrooms, there was nearly always a group of smaller mushrooms. Martha would follow the trail, cutting the stems of an entire colony of mushrooms, letting the smell and the orange-pink colour seep into her fingers. From time to time, she would stand and listen to the wind rustling through the pine trees, knowing that if she stayed quiet no one would find her but also knowing that none of the trees standing in strict formation would provide shelter.

Here in Czawa there were hundreds of different types of mushrooms growing in hidden or half-hidden places, and even under the soil. If she went foraging for mushrooms with Klara, there would be the excitement of eating mushrooms completely unknown to her and the slight uncertainty, despite what Klara said, about whether the mushrooms were edible or not. She stopped and looked up. In the distance, among the trees, stood a tall dark-haired woman dressed in a long coat and a hat in the style of the 1930s. The woman was half-turned away so Martha couldn't see her face. She didn't recognize her, but she knew her. If the woman standing among the trees turned to face Martha, she would unfold like a fan, revealing both Marion Porter and Vera Mrachko, and if she turned back, Martha's grandmother, Martha's mother. Martha turned away and walked fast along the path in the opposite direction. She didn't know if the woman was looking after her, if she had wanted to approach her, if she wanted something. Martha did not turn back in case there was something she wouldn't understand or couldn't give, in case the woman wouldn't let her go.

Magie ohne Hokuspokus
Städte ohne Touris

HIER WOHNTE
MAX RAESENER
JG. 1881
DEPORTIERT 1941
ERMORDET IN
LODZ
HIER WOHNTE
META RAESENER
GEB. LITTMANN
JG. 1895
DEPORTIERT 1941
ERMORDET IN
LODZ
HIER WOHNTE
ASTA RAESENER
JG. 1921
DEPORTIERT 1941
ERMORDET IN
RIGA
CHARLOTT
MAX SH

IV
WINDOWS

For some months after Martha returned to Melbourne, she and Klara spoke once a week, usually on Sunday evenings. The first time Klara rang, she peered into the computer as if looking down a dark tunnel. "I can't see you Martha, is it very dark there? The camera is not on your face." Klara smiled, relieved, when she saw Martha's face. Towards the end of that first, very long conversation, she told Martha she was rereading a book called *Aga Radinsdatter*. Martha hadn't heard of the book nor of the Norwegian author. Klara laughed. She had seen the book on a shelf in nearly every home she visited throughout her childhood. That had been enough to put her off until one afternoon, when she was sixteen and at home alone and bored, she picked up the book and began to read. She read for hours. She read as if the book had been written for her and about her, a version of herself set in another time, in an imaginary, parallel world that existed as a ghost world alongside or inside her daily life. The images entered her dreams and became interwoven with what she did during the day. She began to move like Aga Radinsdatter.

Martha bought the book in its English translation and read it over summer. The novel was set in the middle of the thirteenth century in Norway, where at the age of ten, Aga set off on an expedition with her father to see his ancestral farm before he exchanged it for an estate closer to the valley where they lived. The journey would last several weeks. Aga rode her father's old horse. It was the first time she left the valley she had spent all her life living in. A couple of days after they set out, they spent a night at a shoemaker's house. The wife of the shoemaker unbraided Aga's hair and said it was the most beautiful golden red hair she had ever seen. The following morning just before they left, she gave Aga a pair of shoes made of soft red leather. The shoes were light and a deep red colour that Aga had never seen before. The novel was an account of Aga Radinsdatter's life from this first journey to her time as a student in a convent, her love affair with a reckless young man, her marriage, the birth of her children and her return to the valley amid the tumultuous changes in the world around her. No one Martha knew had ever heard of the novel.

One night, when she had almost finished reading the novel of over six hundred pages, Martha dreamed that she was standing on the edge of a gathering or party. She didn't know the purpose of the gathering and wasn't a part of it. She just stood in a dark corner and observed the large table full of guests. A young woman who had been sitting on the floor in the corridor entered and sat at the table. Everyone noticed her because she should not have been at the table. She opened her mouth as if to speak but instead of words, blood poured out of her mouth, followed by small pieces of flesh or intestine. She continued to spew blood and her insides until her head was covered in blood thick as paint, as if she had turned herself inside out. Then she sat with her eyes closed like a clay figure covered in thick red paint.

Soon after Martha returned to Melbourne, she printed several copies of the photograph of the girl at the window. There were three large prints each with varying levels of brightness and two smaller prints. She laid out the three large prints and compared them to the smaller photographs. Each photograph seemed to leave something out. The pots of red and pink geraniums stood out on the white window ledge in all of them. In the large prints, the girl's face and light brown hair were bigger and seemed brighter but her features were blurrier. Martha put a large print beside a smaller print. She looked from one picture to the other. It was difficult to say if the girl was deep in thought or dreaming about something or worried about her cat or just annoyed with her cat. The more Martha looked at the girl, the more it seemed that she could have belonged to any decade in the last one hundred and fifty years. The appearance of the girl in place of the cat no longer surprised Martha; a girl had been conjured up in place of a cat, a girl appeared in place of a cat, a girl that might have been an apparition. Martha peered more closely at the window in both photographs. She would have liked to see the room behind the girl but both the girl and the lacy white curtain surrounding her blocked any view of the inside. Martha put the most sharply focussed and darkest of the bigger photographs into a frame.

Over the next week, Martha cleared out her large bedroom, which she also used as a study. She washed the white walls and swept the bare floorboards. Then one by one, she brought her furniture and other things back into the room. She hung the photograph of the girl at the window high up on the wall opposite the window and behind her desk so that it was almost impossible to look at the photograph directly. From there, the girl looked down with a slightly surly expression and continued to hold the power to become any number of doubles.

Martha put the folders containing notes and photocopies of material about Marion Porter on the floor beside her desk.

The folders weren't in any particular order and she was often surprised by what she found in one folder or the other. She sat on the floor and went through them. One of two purple folders contained notes about Marion's early life. These notes mostly came from Martha's interview with Marion's only surviving relative, a younger cousin called Hilda Matthews who had attended the National Gallery School with Marion. Hilda was in her late eighties and would tell Martha whatever came into her mind as they spoke and drank tea. Her anecdotes didn't seem to relate much to Marion Porter's life, at least not that Martha could tell, and the stories were hardly ever in response to Martha's questions. Even so, Hilda said they had been close all their lives except for periods when they had lost contact and Hilda thought she might never see or hear from Marion again. It was Hilda who told Martha about Marion's photographs displayed in the window of the beach house in Black Rock. Martha put the folder to one side. Beside it, she put the folder dedicated to the time Marion began to photograph interiors, photographs of windows and doors and the interiors of old hotels and old public buildings. This folder was blue. Inside was a photograph of the lobby of a boarding house. It was a dark tonal photograph; the lines were clean and straight. On one side was the beginning of a staircase with a banister of dark wood and beside it, a forbidding gleaming wooden cupboard that could have contained either linens or a dead body.

Martha had pinned a note to the inside of the blue folder: *In these photographs, the last people who lived in these places, looked after them or made use of them have just left. There is a moment of calm and stillness and then the sense that things are about to shift, to fall apart and disappear, to turn into something else.*

Martha had to work out how she could live in Nadwodom,

this city she had visited and lived in for weeks and months but at times hardly knew at all, as if she had dreamed it and had to struggle to bring it back. She looked through the collection of pamphlets and postcards and objects she had kept secret, even from Klara. She needed a project that would get her to Nadwodom, that would allow her to live in Czawa and stay with Klara. Then she would move into one of the three white adjoining sheds, each with a separate door and a window facing Klara's back garden. The first shed would be a studio for Martha and Klara to work in, the second a place for Martha to sleep and rest and the third a place to store their bikes and tools and the things they collected and wanted to keep.

Window I

One afternoon after school, Martha climbed the first three branches of the tree at the bottom of the garden and looked back at her house instead of looking over the fence into the neighbour's yard or over the rooftops. When she looked back, she saw a dark-haired woman looking out the little window by the back door. She stared, keeping as still as the woman, then dropped to the ground and emerged from the branches. She crept up the steep, back garden towards the back of the house. Usually, she would have jumped and waved, but this time she kept low to the ground. The dark-haired woman, her mother, looked distant, as if she was straining to see something in the horizon. The closer Martha crept to the house, the more distant, the more determined and ferocious her mother seemed. Martha kept low and made her way back to the tree.

Window II

When Marion Porter was twenty-five and had already settled on photography as her medium, she went on her first and only voyage to England to visit family on her father's side. On board the SS Persic, she met a geographer from Czawa. She knew nothing about Czawa, although she had a vague notion that in the Eastern part there was a large area of marshes. She had this idea because as a child she liked to look through the geography books on the bookshelves in the drawing room. Her favourite book was about dwellers on and among waterways throughout the world. She and the geographer often met on deck and as they walked or looked out to sea, he told her about his country's history of partitions and rebellions. He told her about his family's estate in the eastern part of Czawa and described the nearby marshlands and forests and the people who lived in this shifting borderland region.

Early in the voyage, somewhere on the great Australian Bight. there was a storm. Most of the passengers, including the geographer, were seasick. Marion wrote in her notebook: "I had one whole side of the table to myself. I sat in the extreme centre – one small person sitting alone on one side of a huge table. I imagined I was going further north to Czawa. I can see myself one day taking a trip and travelling to the marshlands and outermost areas." She wrote how glad she was to have gotten away from home, grateful that her dad had let her go. Towards the end of the voyage, Marion told the geographer that one day, she would travel to his country to take photographs and learn more about the places he described.

Marion corresponded with the geographer over the next few years and at the age of thirty she organised a trip to Czawa. She planned to carry out a careful and methodical photographic documentation of the countryside with the help of the geographer. She would travel across the countryside by car, photographing and recording the customs, dress, economy and culture of the many ethnic communities. She would only stop briefly in the cities to rest and prepare for the next leg of the journey.

Marion Porter stopped in Nadwodom for a few days. She stayed at the Grand Hotel and met the textile industrialist, Frederik Werner, and his wife Maria. She was shown the factory complex and the hospital and school built for the Werner factory workers and their families. As they left the Werner mansion, Marion looked across the road at the workers' housing. Just before she got back to the car, she ducked into one of the gateways. The geographer, her guide and travelling companion, waited near the car at the end of the street. Marion kept close to the wall of the building and ventured no further than the entrance. She looked up at the tenement and saw a girl's face in a third storey window. The face looked blurry through the grimy, smeared pane, but Marion could see she had a serious and sharp expression on her face, as if she was looking out for someone.

~

In the far left-hand corner, away from the Marion Porter material, Martha arranged two small piles of books. The first pile included the book Klara had bought for her when she had been in Czawa delivering Mrs. K's ashes. It was a translated version of *The Trial* by Kafka. Martha had read it on the farm at the same time as Klara had while she was on the archaeological dig. Klara bought the other two books, written by authors from Czawa, during Martha's most recent visit. The first book, *Summer Days on the Edge of the Marshlands*, had been written in the 1920s. On the front cover was a painting of a man dressed in a coat and hat emerging from a half-opened door. The man was half in and half out of the doorway, and although he looked as if he was about to step into the street, the door he pushed open was an interior door. *Summer Days on the Edge of the Marshlands* was a strange, dream-like autobiography or a collection of extended daydreams set in an isolated country town on the eastern border of Czawa. Martha read this collection carefully, sometimes finding it hard to know where she was or whether she understood the meaning of a passage, worrying she might get lost among individual words. The third book was a novel called *Mushrooms*. This book resonated more strongly with Martha, as if somehow the writer had known that somewhere in the world, someone like Martha would read it. She had found it by chance while Klara was on the other side of the bookshop. Martha had already bought an art book and was ready to leave but while waiting, she decided to browse the display table by the entrance. *Mushrooms* had an abstract cover of rich purples, greens and deep blues. It was written by a woman born in the same year as Martha and was set in a fictional town close to the western border of Czawa. It was described as an anarchic and mystical collection of interwoven stories about characters and events from various times in the town's existence. Klara sidled up and asked Martha what she had found. She took the book, read the back cover and tapped it with her finger. She had heard of the writer although she hadn't read any of her work. She bought the book for Martha but kept it and read it first since Martha was going on a trip to visit other relatives. When Martha finally received *Mushrooms*, she put the book in a plastic bag and packed it away in her suitcase. It was only when she took the book out in Melbourne that she saw that Klara had written on the title page: 'Read this book in Autumn, either yours or mine. Read slowly, so that the words and images can fully take shape and linger before you move on.'

Martha read the two books Klara had bought for her simultaneously and intermittently over months, sometimes going back to sections she had read before and sometimes only reading two or three new pages. She kept a dictionary by her side even though she rarely used it. She had not finished either book, and in this way, both novels were ongoing and never ending and she could return to them over and over until they became books she might have written.

Window III

The girl's father was sick with tuberculosis and it had been several weeks since he had been to work at the factory. All over the city there were strikes, demonstrations and barricades. Workers were protesting the Imperial War. They wanted an eight-hour workday and support for the sick. They wanted independence. The girl was sent to buy bread. She avoided the barricades but as she turned into the city's main thoroughfare, she heard chanting and saw a crowd marching. Demonstrators were carrying placards, red flags and party banners. The girl walked into the crowd. She was tall for her age. Someone handed her a placard condemning the autocracy. She held it high. A moment later, there was a cry and Cossacks on horses burst into the crowd. The girl threw aside the placard and ran into a butcher's shop just as a Cossack on a horse crashed into the shop after her. She dived under the counter then ran out the back into a lane. She ran through the streets and into the gateway, across the courtyard to the entrance of her building. She ran up the stairs into the apartment, then crept to the window and keeping low, peered over the windowsill.

~

Among the second pile of books on the floor in the corner was a book Martha had first seen several months ago when she was browsing through the new acquisitions at the Library. The book had a stark white cover and printed across it on an angle and in thick black lettering was the title, *Threads: The History of a Nuclear Disaster*. Even before she glanced at the blurb on the back cover, she knew the book was about the nuclear accident that had happened fifteen years earlier when she tried but failed to go to Czawa on her own. She looked at the front cover without opening the book then took it back to her desk. The book had only recently been translated into English. It was a collection of stories from, and interviews with people living around or working at the nuclear power plant. The author had conducted many interviews with the local people while the disaster was happening and afterwards, in the weeks, months and even years that followed. Martha considered smuggling the book home just for the night but instead bought her own copy at lunch time. Over the next few weeks, Martha read a narrative each day and began to get a sense of what it might have been like to live with the invisible particles that contaminated everything, that made things glow. People from the surrounding villages and towns could not touch the things they had known all their lives, sometimes forbidden even to touch each other. The disaster, the nuclear explosion that poisoned houses and everything in them, that made villages and forests and grass inaccessible for generations, that made people distrust the food they ate, the air around them, their own bodies, became real.

Martha searched for the notebook from her trip to France. She had written a short poem that traced the movement of people on the street amid a catastrophe. The poem circled around the complete silence of the people gathered in the street who were horrified at their own silence and stunted movement.

At the same time that Martha read the English translation, Klara read the translation of the book published in Czawa.

Neither of them realised until they spoke on the telephone months later. Klara said she had seen the front cover in a bookshop window in Nadwodom. She'd bought the book with a similar sense of urgency and expectation and had read it from cover to cover in one sitting. Klara was fifteen when the nuclear accident occurred. She had been so angry that she vowed that she would always protest the injustice of putting ordinary people's lives in danger.

Window IV

One afternoon, the girl went to the window and saw a strange woman standing just inside the gateway. The woman wore a long dark coat and seemed to be waiting for someone. The girl's mother called out again and told her to hurry up. She was supposed to take a package of food to her aunt. She took her time getting down the stairs and slowly approached the gateway. The woman in the dark coat smiled and motioned for her to stop; she had never seen such fine long hair. She stroked the girl's head and long braid. Then she took a coin out of her pocket and gave it to the girl. The girl understood Russian and a little German, but she could not grasp what the woman was saying. The woman said that many girls must envy her beautiful hair. The girl said she was on an errand. She stepped away as quickly as she could and rushed down the street. Later that evening, she began to feel sick and developed a fever. Over the next two days, her mother anxiously monitored the fever. It didn't seem too bad but even after it passed, the girl was too weak to leave her bed. She was bedridden for ten days. When she finally got up and brushed her hair, clumps of hair fell out. There was so little left that patches of scalp began to show through. She stopped brushing her hair and lay in bed waiting for her strength to return. After a few days, the girl got up again and brushed her hair. It no longer came out in clumps, but it was thin and sparse and never grew back as strong and thick as it had once been.

~

When Martha decided that she had to prepare a way to live in Czawa for at least a few years, she rang Klara to tell her. Before she mentioned her decision, she reminded Klara of the time they visited the Werner villa, of the moment Martha had stopped for a few seconds to take a photograph of a black and white cat lying between the flowerpots on a white window ledge.

"When I looked at the picture later, there was no cat and a girl stood at the window. Something happened as I took the photo. It's as if the cat turned into a girl or the girl was always there but the camera uncovered her."

"What does the girl look like?"

"She has brown hair with a part on the side and that's the strange thing, she could be from any time in the last one hundred and fifty years."

Klara said that something about what Martha told her gave her goosebumps. "Send me a copy of the photo and write all of that down."

They didn't speak for a couple of weeks and then Klara rang and said she got a job working for a researcher investigating the early tenements in the old part of the city. She was helping document the buildings before they got demolished or renovated into something else. She spoke fast, excited and bubbling over. That morning, she rode her bike to work faster and more effortlessly than she had ever ridden before. It was as if she and the bike were one and she had a motor inside her. Just yesterday in some of the oldest buildings, they had found some distinctive porches, the type of porches used by Orthodox Jews at Sukkot. Somehow, they had survived. The walls surrounding the tenements were covered in anti-Semitic soccer graffiti that made no sense, but inside the courtyards, the porches were still there. Klara had contacted the Jewish Information Office and they would be working on the project together. "This is part of our project," Klara said.

Window V

Marion Porter returned to the tenement looking for the girl. She took several photographs of the narrow courtyard and then turned to the third storey window. A cat lay on the ledge just inside the window. She wondered whether to enter the building but stopped short when it came to knocking on the door. She quickly put away her camera and left. When the girl looked down from behind the curtain, she saw the strange woman with a bag slung around her torso. The woman had a large camera and photographed the courtyard. Then she looked up and aimed the camera at the window. The girl stepped back and pulled the cat in, off the ledge. The woman turned and rushed out of the courtyard as if she didn't want to be seen.

~

A large lemon tree grew beside the light green weatherboard bungalow that Aunt Mary used to live in. It was a weatherboard bungalow of the type erected in suburban Melbourne backyards in the late 1950s and early 1960s. Aunt Mary had painted the door and window frames a cream colour. Martha sat back in her chair and looked out the window at the bright blue sky. She remembered hearing that the bungalow had been built for Uncle Daniel's father but that he only lived in it for one year. He died a year after it was built and a year before Martha was born. She had heard that he was a quiet, gentle man, and that when his heart stopped in the concentration camp and Uncle Daniel brought him back to life, he asked, "Why did you bring me back to this?" She knew that he and his son had been separated from his wife and daughter who had been killed as soon as they arrived at the camp.

The last time Martha saw the bungalow was just before her aunts moved into a nursing home. The bungalow seemed miniature, as if it was a playhouse. Inside were neatly stacked newspapers, magazines and books. There was a large wardrobe, a chest of drawers and evenly stacked piles of sewing material. Rolls of thicker fabrics stood beside a dressmaker's dummy. Now she imagined a small light green weatherboard bungalow only as tall as a person. The windows had half-drawn blinds and it was possible to glimpse piles of books, journals and richly coloured crimson, purple, blue and green woven fabrics. The door could only be opened a crack, just wide enough to see what was inside but not enough to put an arm in to touch anything or to take anything out. A card on the wall at the entrance to the room in the bungalow, read: "light escapes and shadows speak."

A tree laden with yellow lemons stands next to the scaled down bungalow. The citrus scent is strong, as if the tree has just been watered. There are two identical bungalows set up in the same way and shown at the same time on either side of the world. One is in the Museum of Modern Art in Nadwodom and the other is in the Institute of Contemporary Art in Melbourne.

~

Dearest Martha,

Snow is falling over absolutely all Czawa. Winter has come suddenly and sharply. Everything looks very clean and light and soft. I think you would like this weather.

Klara

Window VI

From the end of the room, as far away from the window as she could be while still seeing through it, the mother looked out and down into the courtyard. Her son ran in through the entrance. A moment later, she heard him pounding up the stairs. She opened the door just wide enough for him to get through. He pulled off his brown sheepskin coat and she buried it in the old iron box where they kept coal. He ran into the bedroom and she hid him under the feather bedding. She sat on top of the bedclothes. The soldiers entered the flat. He was wanted on two accounts; he was a teacher and he had refused to relinquish the coat. The younger sister let them in and said her mother was sick. They asked for a man wearing a brown sheepskin coat. They wanted to know if a teacher lived here and if they knew where he was. The girl said no such person lived in the apartment. They searched every room, looked in the cupboards and entered the bedroom. The mother sat on the bed and did not utter a word. The soldiers left. From that day, the mother stopped speaking, as if something had been clamped down so hard it couldn't be opened again. Sometimes she sang softly, either to herself or to whoever was speaking to her.

Two months later, the girl stood at the window and watched her mother leave the courtyard with a bundle of food under her arm. It was the beginning of winter but already icy. Every morning, her mother went to the gates of the military headquarters where they had imprisoned her son. She hoped to get just a glimpse of him and a chance to throw him the food. She did this for over a week and never once saw him. One morning as she trudged back, she slipped on the icy road and fell. She broke her arm and shoulder. The girl sat beside her mother's bed. She didn't like to sit for so long, but her mother gazed at her the whole time so that she couldn't move.

~

Martha sat at her desk with her back to the framed photograph of the girl at the window. She couldn't decide which print to send to Klara and she didn't want to send the image electronically. A transformation had taken place and it had to be handled with care. She made up her mind to take all the prints of the photograph to Nadwodom so that she and Klara could look at them together, side by side. Martha looked down at the shiny, varnished, green wooden ring on her left middle finger. It was the same vivid green as the tops of the bushes she could see outside her window. She and Klara bought one ring each from a stall at the marketplace in the village, by the river where Martha's mother and her friends had once gone swimming. Green bushes, green rings, green forest and woodlands. That day Klara's mother came with them and looked mournful as she reminisced about the summers she had spent with her older sister when they were young.

Martha and Klara had walked away from Klara's mother to look at the stall selling wooden jewellery. There were rows and rows of varnished wooden rings in all colours. Martha picked up a golden yellow one and a crimson one and then tried on the bright green one. Klara picked up a dark green ring. It fit her middle finger perfectly. They bought the rings and put them on straight away. Klara had laughed and said, "You will come and live here." And Martha knew that she would, that they would live out their old age together side by side even though it was not clear to her exactly where they would live. Now Martha sat at her desk and looked at the varnished green ring on her middle finger and thought of Klara, believing that Klara would sense her thoughts. She saw herself standing at the upstairs bedroom window in the house on the edge of the forest reserve in Nadwodom. Through the trees she saw two distant figures, herself and Klara.

Late that night, a girl with large eyes appeared in the corner of Martha's room. The girl stood motionless and staring. Her eyes were black and hollow and grew steadily bigger until they became like caverns threatening to obliterate her face. Martha gathered all her strength to turn away and look up at the ceiling. The ceiling was close, close enough to breathe on. She turned her head and looked down at the bed below. Her body lay on one side of the bed and Klara lay on the other. They lay facing each other like crescents or brackets enclosing the crumpled sheet. Martha let herself fall and felt her cheek sink into the pillow. The house was quiet and dark. She lay immersed in silence, like floating in a lake in the middle of the night.

Photo courtesy of Hannah Raszewski-Barkhoff

MONICA RASZEWSKI was born in Melbourne and currently works as a librarian at the University of Melbourne. She has had short fiction published in Australian literary journals and anthologies and has had several stage plays performed in Melbourne and Sydney. Her radio plays have been produced by the ABC (Australian Broadcasting Corporation) and broadcast nationally.

Monica received a State Library of Victoria Creative Fellowship to write her most recent play, *There are Trees that are Dancers*, which was awarded a Ross Trust Playwrights' Development Award and was performed at The Courthouse Theatre (La Mama).

Photo courtesy of Zan Wimberley

JANE E. BROWN's landscapes and interiors are characterized by atmospheres of seduction and melancholy. Carefully observed scenes from around the world hold a distinct anthropological charge, exploring absence, chance and the materiality of time.

Hand printed in her own darkroom, her generally small-scaled, gelatin silver photographs bring an eccentric and elegiac eye to her subjects. As well as literary influences her work engages with the history of photography, the melancholy of experience and the emotional resonance of place.

Jane is an award-winning artist and professional photographer. Her work is held in the collections of the National Gallery of Victoria, the Art Gallery of New South Wales and the Southeast Museum of Photography, Florida, USA. Born in Al Ahmadi, Kuwait, Jane lives and works in Melbourne, Australia.

www.ingramcontent.com/pod-product-compliance
Lightning Source LLC
Chambersburg PA
CBHW020807190726
48285CB00006B/2185